Cypathia

Part One: The Secret Princess

by

Teresa Clyne

Disclaimer

Cypathia Copyright © 2015 by Teresa Clyne.

Cover design by Steve De La Mare

Reader Loyalty BONUS…!!

Part Two: Reunited -Absolutely FREE....!!

For my children, Stacey, Davie, Mark and Kerri, grandbabies, Evan, Makenzie, Sierrah, Alexie and Harper, who taught me about family, unconditional love and to trust, my most trusted friends who supported me since forever and Mrs. McGee, for whom I would not be the person I am today.

Part One

The Secret Princess

Chapter 1

"READY, AIM, FIRE!" screamed the King as a cloud of smoke swirled across the artillery battery.

The sound of falling stone was deafening as the battlements fell and the castle walls were breached. The Queen looked at her husband with wide eyes. Her heart was pounding in her chest; feeling like it would leap right out of her body. Her long red curly hair was now looking white from the dust which was covering everything in the castle. The noise was deafening and hurt her ears, her mind was a whirl of thoughts, and she was trying to take everything that was happening in and making sense of it. A blast of air came through one of the shattered windows and hit her in the face, jolting her back to reality

"Teddy, PLEASE get the minders and go to the portal," Alexander ordered. "It's time."

"No! I won't leave you," Theodora shouted, tears streaming down her face.

Alexander flinched as another huge bang caused the floor to vibrate under his feet. "You have to go my darling. Think of the children. Get them to safety."

Theodora threw herself into her husband's arms and he squeezed her back in a big bear hug before pushing her back and taking her by the hands. "Go now!" he told her giving her hands a final squeeze, "I will find you and the children in Kaleseth later when the fighting is over." Everything seemed to move fast yet slow at the same time. The sound of arrows impacting with the castle windows was enough for Alexander to shout at Theodora, "Teddy, GO… NOW."

With enormous strength of will, he turned away from her so he could concentrate on the battle. Theodora wiped her eyes determinedly and set off to find the minders. She knew Alexander was right. She had to get her children to safety. Kaia was the heiress to the Kingdom of Cypathia and if King Mordor captured her during this war, there would be no future for her people.

Theodora hurried through the castle as quickly as she could in her flowing skirts. After tripping twice, she bundled them up in her hands so she could move faster. She burst into the twin's nursery, breathless and panting. "Catherine, Isadora, it's time," she said.

Both guardians gulped and nodded their heads with grim expressions on their faces. Each scooped up a squirming, wriggling bundle and walked towards the door without a word. The three ladies made their way through the maze of corridors and down stone steps until they reached the bottom floor of the castle. The portal had been set up in an unused room far away from the hustle and bustle. The King and Queen had not wanted to risk its discovery and word of their plans leaked to their enemies.

"Are you ready?" Catherine asked.

"No," Theodora replied, "I don't want to leave without my husband," shaking her head vehemently. "Not now not ever, can we not just wait here for him until the battle is over?"

"Ma'am," began Catherine tentatively, "the battle will not be over for hours and it isn't safe here. We cannot wait any longer. King Mordor will come soon and if he captures the babies…" All of them knew what that would mean.

"But, but…" Theodora stammered, "Ok, I suppose Alexander will just meet us in Kaleseth later like he said." Catherine and Isadora looked at each other in alarm. Both the guardians were more than just simple nannies. Catherine was a powerful sorceress, a slightly overweight, petite, brown eyed woman with chestnut hair resting neatly on her shoulders and Isadora was her apprentice. When the battle was imminent, the palace had searched far and wide for the best protector in the land. The twins had just been born and King Alexander had feared for their safety. His most trusted knight had set off on his horseback to find the right person for the job. When he hadn't returned in a fortnight, the King had feared the worst – that he had been captured. But just two days later, the knight had come storming over the castle's drawbridge with news that he had found people willing to take on the task of protecting the babies.

Catherine and Isadora had been summoned to the castle and they had begun working on their plan. That had been six months ago. They had worked day and night perfecting the portal – a means to transport the twins to safety, somewhere far away, should war break out. In close consultation with the King and Queen, they had decided on the Realm of Kaleseth where the twins would grow up and hopefully return back to Cypathia when Kaia was of age to ascend to the throne.

In Cypathia the first born child to the King and Queen rose to power at thirteen years of age. As Kaia, whose name meant wise child, had arrived two minutes before Kolby, named for the head full of dark hair he was born with, she was the rightful heiress to the Kingdom of Cypathia.

King Alexander had been so worried about his children that he had privately pleaded with Catherine to put some kind of fail-safe into effect as an extra protection. "If we can simply slip through a portal into another realm, then there is nothing stopping King Mordor from doing the same. There must be some kind of spell you can put on the portal to stop him from following us through," he had said.

And so, Catherine had gone back to work and the only thing she had been able to find was a locking spell. The first part of the spell had to be woven into the portal when it was created. Once they were through to safety, she would perform the second part of the spell which would lock the portal for twelve years. It would only be able to be re-opened at sunrise on the twins' thirteenth birthday and not before. The King had been very specific in his orders, "make sure there is no dark magic that can break through the barrier that protects my family from evil. Under no circumstances must you tell Teddy. She will never agree to go and leave me behind. You MUST promise!" he had insisted.

Reluctantly Catherine had set about creating the portal and weaving into it the locking spell that would cause the passage between the realms to collapse for twelve years. She worked with a heavy heart, hating to deceive her Queen, but she knew it was for the best. The portal was the most advanced piece of magic she had ever performed and Isadora had been nervous and wary, constantly asking, "what if something goes wrong?" Catherine had shushed her and soothed her fears every time, but now as they stood about to enter the portal, Catherine had to admit her tummy was also in churning.

Isadora had come to Catherine as an apprentice quite by accident. She was very young when her parents had fallen very sick. Catherine had been called by a neighbour to try and heal them but it had been too late, even for her special kind of magic, to save them. She had done her best but after a few hours had to admit defeat. She had been explaining to the neighbour that there was nothing more she could do for them when she had heard a sniffing noise coming from the corner of the room. She'd looked over to see a filthy waif of a girl cowering in the corner, small in stature with the blondest hair parted in the middle, porcelain skin and the most expressive blue eyes the like of which Catherine had never seen before. Her eyes were wide, staring out from a tear and dirt-streaked face. Catherine could not leave this tiny waif without finding out who was going to take care of her.

She had asked the neighbour if there were any family who she could contact to send the girl to, but the neighbour had told her that there was nobody, fearing that Catherine would suggest that she take the child in and take care of her, the neighbour hurriedly left, muttering under her breath "I have enough of my own children who I can barely feed let alone take on another one" Catherine heard her murmuring but understood completely. Catherine had far too soft a nature to leave a child to fend for them self and had taken her in. From that day, she had raised Isadora as her own and it had become clear, very soon, that Isadora had what they called "the sight." Catherine had set about training her to be a sorceress too, but Isadora had an impulsive nature and was impatient and this often lead to mishaps over the cauldron, most mishaps were often quite funny.

Isadora was a curious and impatient apprentice, tapping her fingers on the wooden sideboard which stood tall next to the cauldron, never wanting to wait for spells and potions to mature which often resulted in unfinished potions and incomplete spells, "for the last time Isadora, you must wait for the potions to mature in the cauldron before you remove the potions and put them in the viles," groaned Catherine. Isadora knew that Catherine was right, of course, as she sheepishly hung her head, "I'm sorry Catherine, truly I am, but I feel that am I never going to be a sorceress?" "My dear child," Catherine said as she gently tapped Isadora's shoulder and handing her a tissue for her welled up eyes, "you are already a great sorceress, you just need to learn patience and believe in yourself, now compose yourself child."

Now, more than twenty five years later, Isadora was still nervous of her ability and tended to be clumsy and impulsive. While she had mastered the basics of spell-making, she was unable to progress because she didn't have confidence in herself. It frustrated Catherine greatly as she knew that Isadora had exceptional ability if only she would just believe in herself. She had long given up trying to get Isadora to work as an independent sorceress. They were a great team as they were and Isadora preferred Catherine to take the lead with her being second in command. It was an arrangement that suited them both and it was how they had both ended up at the castle when the King had only been looking for one guardian.

"What's wrong?" demanded the Queen, snapping Catherine out of her daydream and back to the present moment. Catherine sighed. "This is why I don't like secrets," she said, "They always cause more trouble than they're worth."

Chapter 2

An inquisitive look swept across the Queen's face. "What do you mean 'secrets' Catherine?" asked the Queen. "You had better tell me what's going on right now!" Catherine and Isadora knew that they had to tell the Queen the truth about the escape through the portal.

Catherine and Isadora set about trying to explain the locking spell and making Queen Theodora understand that Alexander would not be joining them after the battle was over. As they spoke, Theodora dropped to her knees, one hand clutching her heart and the other steadying her on the wall "HOW COULD HE DO THIS?" she screeched hysterically.

"I don't want to leave him and I don't want to leave my babies either. How can I possibly choose between the two most important things in my life?" She started to sob, tears streaming down her cheeks, rivulets of tears made from the beige dust which was coving the Queen from head to toe. She wrestled with the hardest decision she had ever had to make

Isadora, the more compassionate of the guardians dropped to her knees too, carefully cradling Kaia in the one arm and put her other arm around the Queen. "Ma'am, it's for the best. King Alexander wants you to be safe too. We must go now. Can you hear? The battle sounds are drawing nearer. Soon it will be too late," she pleaded.

"NO!" Theodora shouted. "This is unacceptable!" She stood up with a determined expression on her face. "I cannot go without him. You two wait here for me, I'm going to get him and we will all go together." And with that she spun on her heel and marched off back down the corridor.

Catherine and Isadora stared after her with wide open mouths and before either of them could do a thing to stop her she was gone from sight. Isadora started to panic. The shouts and cries of the warriors were getting louder with each passing second which meant that they didn't have time to waste. She turned to Catherine, who was like a mother to her and her eyes filled with tears. Catherine was afraid too but she knew if she showed fear in front of the panicking Isadora that this would make the situation worse. She composed herself as best she could, try to balance her breathing so as to give the pacing Isadora an air of confidence. Isadora stopped pacing and stood in front of Catherine.

"What are we going to do?" she asked in a high pitched voice that was bordering on hysterical. "Should we wait? Should we go? What if we make the wrong decision? Oh why did we get ourselves into this mess?"

Catherine grabbed her by the arm, "Isadora, you have to calm down. If you go into the portal in such a state, you know things can go wrong. You have to clear your mind and focus now."

"How can you expect me to calm down?" Isadora shrieked back at her and with that Kaia began to cry. The wailing baby seemed to bring Isadora back to what was important and she lowered her voice and spoke in a soothing tone to quiet her down. She was rocking Kaia and asking Catherine in a furious whisper what they were going to do, when around the corner burst Sir Galdo, the King's most trusted knight. He was dirty and bloody from the battle and had a crazed look. Catherine stepped forward immediately. "Sir Galdo, what's the matter? Please tell me the King is alright?"

"For now," Sir Galdo replied hastily. "We are managing to hold them back but barely. Their reinforcements will be here before ours so it's a matter of time before the castle walls fall. The King sent me to make sure you had gone through the portal and were safe. What on earth are you waiting for?"

"Her Majesty told us to wait. She did not want to leave the King behind," Catherine replied, "She has gone back to fetch him."

Sir Galdo was so shocked that he could not form words for a few seconds. "She did WHAT?" he bellowed. "The King is going to be FURIOUS! Are you two not meant to be the royal protectors?"

At that Isadora, impulsive as ever, stepped forward and jabbed him on the chest with her finger. "Excuse me?" she demanded. "I don't know who you think you are. We tried our best, but Her Majesty is an incredibly determined woman and once she had made up her mind, there was nothing we could do to stop her, most especially since we are holding the babies. What would you have had us do – wrestle the Queen to the floor and hold her down against her will?"

"Isadora, stop rambling," Catherine told her. "What's done is done. The question now Sir Galdo is, what do we do now?"

"You activate the portal immediately and get yourself and the children through it," he said. "I will go and find the Queen and make sure she is taken to a place of safety until the battle is over. You have to go now! The King needs to focus on keeping the castle walls standing and he cannot do that if he has to also worry about his wife and children."

Another loud bang erupted and a halo of dust fell down on top of Kolby causing him to sneeze. Sir Galdo looked at the roof meaningfully. "You see, no time to wait. Get going or you are going to answer to the wrath of the King when you have to explain how you two allowed his children to be captured." Isadora was pacing in tight circles, the floor boards creaking under her pacing feet, Catherine looked at Isadora with a frown so stern that both of her eyebrows met in the middle over the bridge of her nose.

"Right," said Catherine. "Let's get going." She turned to Isadora, "take a deep breath and visualize where we are going. Make a clear picture in your mind. Remember I taught you how to clear your mind and keep the picture clear throughout the journey? It will only take a few seconds but it will feel like longer as you are pulled and stretched through time to the other realm. Do not let go of Kaia or she will be lost in time forever. You can do this Isadora – just keep your eyes on my aura and follow it through the portal – it will be a bright purple trail in the darkness."

Isadora took a deep breath and steadied herself. Her mind was all over the place with everything that was happening, but she knew she needed to focus. "I'm ready," she told her mentor and friend and then silently added "I hope," to herself.

With that Catherine began waving her hand over a place in the stone and chanting.

"Alakazam, Alakzelm,
Open the portal to the Kaleseth realm,
Keep us safe around every bend,
Then lock the door at our journey's end"

Over and over Catherine said the spell until a bright purple light came out of her hand and joined with the stones. The purple spread up the stones to the roof and down to the floor until a shimmering curtain of silk stood before them in the wall. "I'm going in now Isadora, you follow after me, straight away – don't wait," Catherine instructed.

Isadora was so tense, she could only nod in agreement and then she watched Catherine and Kolby disappear through the wall. "Right this is it," Isadora thought. "Show time!"

She stepped forward into the curtain and felt something sucking her in. She held onto Kaia tightly and forced herself to open her eyes and look for the purple trail. She felt like she was being pulled and stretched out of shape as she made her way after the purple trail – it was the strangest sensation ever! Going through the curtain was like trying to swim through something sticky like treacle, and then it felt like the space surrounding her was getting thicker until it felt like she was trying to move through bread dough before it was baked. It was getting warmer inside the portal and she wiped her brow with her free hand, still clutching Kaia tightly with the other.

She adjusted to the feeling after a few seconds and then began to relax. "I've got this under control," she thought happily, but then disaster struck.

Kaia began to scream. The baby was clearly not enjoying the funny feeling of the portal and was getting more distressed by the second. Isadora looked down at her in alarm and frantically tried to reassure her that everything was going to be alright, but Kaia was having none of it. When Isadora looked up again, the purple trail from Catherine's aura was gone....

Chapter 3

Isadora panicked. She looked all around and suddenly felt disorientated and scared, dazed for a few minutes, it felt like her head was heavy. Kaia was still crying and she clung to the baby for dear life. She turned around; not knowing which way was forward anymore.

"No, no, no, no, no, NOOOOOOOO!" she shouted. "Am I going to be lost in time forever?"
Awful thoughts swirled in her head of staying stuck in this time warp for the rest of eternity and she started to cry too. After a few seconds she realized that she had to pull herself together or she would never get out of this mess. She had to concentrate, so she cleared her head as best she could. Now what was she supposed to visualize again? Waterfalls? Forests? Big open fields? "Think Isadora" she said to herself.

It was times like these where she wished she had more patience in those classes and paid more attention to Catherine but to be honest, she certainly hadn't thought that things would get so bad that Cypathia would end up at war with King Mordor. And even on the rare occasion that she had allowed herself to think that there might be a chance, never once had she imagined being separated from Catherine and having to figure this all out on her own.

"Okay, no time for that now," she thought. "Let me clear my mind and try to relax. I'm sure that's what Catherine said."

And slowly, Isadora felt herself being sucked forwards again and the darkness started to lighten. "Thank goodness," Isadora thought with relief, "this could have been a total disaster."

As she neared the end of the portal journey, she squeezed her eyes shut tightly against the strange feeling. The light shining through her eyelids got brighter and it felt as if she was being squeezed out of a tube. With a loud pop, she crashed down on top of something hard and heard the clattering of knives, forks and plates. Isadora was disorientated for an instant and rapidly everything came back to normal, she inhaled two really deep breaths and looked around trying to get her bearings.

"Uh oh!" she thought. She tentatively opened one eye and gasped in shock. She had landed right in the middle of someone's dinner table – while they were eating! Isadora blinked frantically, trying to get her eyes to adjust to the sudden bright light and as she looked around she saw seven pairs of eyes blinking back at her in astonishment.

"What in blazes is going on here?" roared the man at the head of the table as he dropped his turkey drumstick down on his plate and pushed his chair back from the table. While he was a slightly built man, he had a powerful voice and Isadora was afraid.

"Cripes!" Isadora squeaked. She had to think fast. Quickly she grabbed the magic amulet that hung around her neck and pointed it at the room.

"HOCUS POCUS, KAPIZZ KAPOW,
Stop the world, freeze time NOW!"

As she chanted the spell a trail of silver mist shot out of the amulet and settled like a blanket over everyone at the dinner table, freezing them immediately. "Okay, think Isadora!" she commanded herself.

This was a disaster. She had no idea where she was and she was almost positive she was nowhere near Catherine. Then she had an awful thought. If she could so easily land in the wrong place, maybe she had disrupted everything by landing in the wrong time too. If she had somehow travelled through time she would have messed with the entire course of history, changing it forever.

She climbed carefully off the table, still holding Kaia, and started looking around the room for a clue as to where she was. After about five minutes of frantic searching, she found a news scroll tucked down the side of the sofa. She set Kaia down carefully with a cushion behind her head and shook out her hands anxiously. She grabbed the scroll with shaking fingers and unrolled it slowly to see the date.

Isadora nearly cried with relief when she saw that it was yesterday's news scroll. So at least she was in the right time zone! She unrolled the scroll a little further and sank down to her knees in utter shock. There in black and white read the headlines…

Herecian Knight qualifies for Inter-Realm Jousting Tournament

"Herecia!" Isadora shrieked. "How could I have landed up in…in Herecia?!" She jumped up looking around the room for the portal opening so they could go back through it and try to find Catherine in Kaleseth. But even as she frantically tried to find the portal, she knew the truth – they were stuck here for the next twelve years. She went over to where Kaia was lying and scooped the baby into her arms.

"I'm sorry. I'm so sorry," she said over and over again. "I'll try find a way to put things right, somehow."

No worse the wear after the portal journey Kaia gurgled and stretched and kicked her legs. She nuzzled into Isadora and gave a happy sigh. Isadora was comforted by the fact that at least she had Kaia with her and could keep her safe. She vowed to do everything in her power to keep the princess out of harm's way so that they would find the portal opening on her thirteenth birthday.

Isadora sprang to action, her mind abuzz with ideas to explain their presence to the family whose dinner they had landed on. Finally she decided that since she knew nobody in Herecia the easiest thing would be to stay with the family they had accidentally landed with. Isadora knew she would have to perform a powerful spell to pull it off for twelve years but she had never been more determined.

She opened the heavy wooden door at the back of the kitchen and gingerly stuck her head out. She breathed in the fresh air and started to feel a bit calmer. She couldn't deny Herecia was beautiful. In the distance she saw rolling green hills, with valleys in-between which were home to the most magnificent lakes and tree lined rivers, Isadora stepped outside properly, she turned to look at the house from which she had just come. It was a simple stone house with a thatched roof and two floors. Green vines wove their way up the stone and decorated the outside walls with beautiful white flowers, the gardens housed the most beautiful roses and lilies Isadora had ever seen, the smell of roses mixed with lilies was exquisite. Looking to the left and right of her, most of the houses in the area seemed to be the same. She was standing in a rather large garden and down in the furthest corner she saw a stone wall. It was very high, almost as if it was hiding something behind it.

She made her way down to the wall and found the opening round the side. The sight that greeted her made her smile. There stood a small quaint little cottage; it looked completely square with a steep red roof, Isadora remembered having a beehive in Cypathia that she was reminded of when she glimpsed at the cottage. It was a little run down but she was sure she would be happy living there and at least the wall gave her a bit of privacy.

She went back up to the house and prepared to put her plan into action. She found a laundry basket and set Kaia down on top of a bundle of freshly laundered clothes and took a deep breath. She had seen Catherine perform these kinds of spells hundreds of times but had never done one all alone before. She was nervous because her timing had to be perfect. As she unfroze everyone, she had to immediately perform the memory spell, before the family realized what was happening. If she got it wrong their memories would be spliced and they would all go mad. The memory spell itself was simple. The complicated part was that she had to get all seven people with the spell at the same time. Memories of the last spell came back to her in a flash, she clenched her fist so tight her knuckles turned white, she felt paralysed, "pull yourself together Isadora," she thought to herself as she bit the right side of her bottom lip, feeling vulnerable yet determined.

Isadora positioned herself in front of the table her hands shaking with both fear and apprehension; she removed the amulet from around her neck. As she clicked her fingers to unfreeze the family, she began her spell.

Change their memories, make them forget,
That Kaia and I aren't part of the family yet.
Let them welcome us into their home,

So we don't have to spend the next twelve years alone.

Make the years speed by in a flash,

Alakazam, Alakazim, Alakabash!

As she shouted the last three words, light rays shot out her fingers and hit each member of the family square in the middle of the forehead. They all looked wide eyed and stunned and for a panicked moment Isadora also worried that she had somehow got the spell wrong. But as they snapped back to reality, the mother shouted, "Isadora, clear these plates away immediately."

Isadora breathed a sigh of relief, scurried over to the table and hurriedly started gathering up the dishes. As she dumped them in the sink, she heard the loud bang of a fist coming down and pounding the table. Isadora jumped and spun around quickly to see what the matter was.

"Isadora!!!" screeched the long dark-haired woman. "What on earth is the baby doing in the laundry basket? I thought I told you she was to remain in the attic during meal times!"

"Sorry Ma'am," stammered Isadora, "She was crying and I thought it would give her comfort to be near us all."

"I don't allow you to stay here and work for us so that you can give me your opinion on how you think things should be," the well-kempt woman continued, "I give you free lodging to do as you're told. Now get her out of here. You can finish the dishes in the morning."

"Yes Ma'am," Isadora replied and quickly scooped up Kaia and left the kitchen to search for the attic room. She would have to do a quick bit of magic to get it looking like a nursery should look - with a crib for the baby.

As she made her way up the stairs, she peered into the rooms to get an idea of what kind of décor she would need to make the attic fit in with the rest of the house. The house was simple and a little messy. You could see the family wasn't rich and that their furniture had been passed down through the generations. Still it was homely and Isadora had a better idea of what she would need to do.

She climbed the last flight of steps and opened up the attic trapdoor. She stepped into the grimiest, dingiest room she thought she had ever seen. The only decoration was cobwebs that stretched the length of the room and a thick layer of dust covered the walls and floor. "Why on earth do they want to keep their baby up here?" she wondered out loud to herself.

"Oh well, never mind that now, she said to Kaia. "Time to get this place spruced up for you princess." And with that she set about casting spells this way and that to clean up the room.

When she was done, she set Kaia into the crib and began to gently rock her to sleep singing her favourite lullaby. It wasn't long before the exertions of the day had taken their toll on the little baby and she was sound asleep.

Isadora slumped down on the wooden floor next to the crib, her back leaning against the wall. It was going to be a long twelve years!

Chapter 4

Kaia ducked as a clay pot whizzed past her, missing her head by inches. She turned quickly and trembled as she watched it shatter into hundreds of pieces just before it hit the stone wall behind her. Luckily Endor, her mother, was in such a rage that she didn't notice. It wouldn't do with the mood she was in to have any more strange things happen that she couldn't explain. Kaia had no idea why these funny things seemed to happen to her and she had no way of explaining them. She only knew that when she was angry or upset weird things, like clay pots shattering in mid-air, seemed to happen. At first it was just the occasional thing, but as she had gotten older, the incidents had started becoming more frequent. Just the other day she had almost set fire to the house when her eldest brother Ralph had sat at the table flicking bits of stale bread at her while she scrubbed the kitchen floor. As each piece of bread hit her, Kaia felt her irritation grow and before she knew what was happening the lantern had burst and flames were rushing across the table to where he sat. Luckily Isadora had been doing the washing up and had thrown a pot of water onto the flames before they could do any real damage. Isadora was the only person she could talk to about it, and she was none the wiser as to why these things were happening either.

"Get out of my sight, you ungrateful little imp!" screeched Endor, as she looked around for something else to toss at Kaia. Kaia crossed her arms in stubborn defiance, but Endor was angry and determined. Endor lunged towards Kaia with venom in her voice, "get out" she hissed, causing Kaia to slump into an unhappy silence, she didn't need to be told twice. She scooped up Billow, her pet dragon, and bolted out of the kitchen door. Once in the safety of the garden, she gave a loud sigh. She really had the worst luck. Her mother had been in bed for three days and had to pick the exact moment when she was having a moan to decide to get up and come through to the kitchen.

"I suppose I should know better," she told Billow, giving his fluffy white feathers a stroke, "But honestly, that's the UGLIEST dress I have ever seen! Not even the street urchins at the market place wear such hideous clothes!"

Billow looked up at Kaia like he knew exactly what she was talking about. Kaia ranted on; now safely out of ear shot of her mother. "I can't believe Edith gave me that awful orange and brown dress and told me it was a birthday gift. Firstly, my birthday isn't for another week, not that I expected anything mind you. Nobody has ever given me a birthday gift before. Now mother says I have to wear it or she is going to give me a good hiding. What am I going to do Billow?" Kaia lamented.

Billow purred as Kaia stroked him on his favourite spot between his budding wings and a small puff of smoke shot out of his nostrils. Kaia looked down at her pet with affection. He was more than just a pet or even a friend. He was her soul mate. Sometimes Kaia felt that he was the only one who understood her. Isadora was great and she always had Kaia's back, but Kaia just couldn't seem to shake the feeling that there was something the older woman was keeping from her.

Billow was the only thing she had ever truly wanted that she had been allowed to keep. If she ever showed even the slightest interest in anything, including food, you could be sure that someone in her family would take it from her. She had spent a good portion of her early years in an incredible state of hunger because she had not yet learned how to be indifferent when dinner time came. Her eagerness to tuck in had often meant she was banished to the attic and only ever given cold left overs and that was on a really lucky day. Most days she went to bed clutching her tummy against the rumbling and cramps. As she got older she realized that if she was going to be allowed any table scraps, she had to act like she wasn't hungry at all and slowly she had perfected the art. None of the kids ever got given any meat to eat. Meat was solely for her father, Iosaf, and her mother, on the rare occasion she was well enough to be out of bed. Kaia would often salivate watching Iosaf tear huge chunks of meat off turkey drumsticks and long for the day she would be allowed to eat one. She soon learned that day was never going to come.

But Kaia was clever and she had quickly learned a few tricks that had gotten her through childhood. She usually the one given the worst household chores, especially now that she was older and Maude and Priscilla had married and moved out. She used to make sure that she was the one to clear the dinner dishes from the table and if she was really lucky, she was able to pull off the scraps of turkey from the bone that her father hadn't finished. Occasionally there was even a potato and the odd piece of vegetable. If she was quick and careful, she could gobble them up before anyone noticed. But mostly the kids were fed bread. This wouldn't have been so bad if the bread was fresh and tasty and had a delicious homemade preserve on as a topping, but generally, it was a few days old, too old for her father and only then was it deemed alright to give to the kids. No butter, no jam, just plain, stale bread and a little water.

Luckily for Kaia not every day was filled with hunger, one hot sunny Sunday afternoon Kaia and Billow were coming home from another exploring mission when one of her neighbours Mr. Thayer called her, "Kaia, come here child," Kaia liked Mr. Thayer and skipped over to see why he wanted to speak to her, he was holding a small wicker basket, "here child, take these and give them to Isadora, we had lots of eggs left over this week, our chickens have laid way too many eggs, and these did not sell in market" he said as he handed the basket to Kaia, "Mr. Thayer, oh thank you, I do love eggs," she knew that they were not left over as Kaia often heard Mr. Thayer say how they could have done with more eggs at the market, they never had enough, Mr. Thayer once told the butcher that Kaia was never given enough to eat, he remarked "she always looks so peaky and thin."   Kaia shook Mr. Thayer's hand excitedly "Thank you Mr. Thayer" as she turned on her heel and rushed in to give the eggs to Isadora.

Kaia had often remarked how her neighbours were an odd mixture, strange and even excitable. From the excitable Napoleon's next door, with 8 boys who were all as wild as feral cats to the Weavers who only seemed to leave the house at night, Mr and Mrs Thayer were an older couple, they had no children, Mr. Thayer always wore a blazer and peak cap, even in the hot summers, he always kept a pipe in his mouth, and puff the most divine smelling smoke right up into the air, Mrs. Thayer was a short woman, with long white hair, she often wore a dress that reminded Kaia of the flour bags that Isadora kept in the pantry, but Kaia knew that Mrs. Thayer hardly wore a flour sack so she dismissed this thought, Mrs. Thayer also smoked but the smell of her smoke was rancid. Ms. Paxon lived right next door to the right, a rather angry old lady who always wore a bright red hat and a black fur coat every time she left the house, she hissed "*gabachio*" at Kaia every time she walked by her house, Kaia was unsure what gabachio even meant or why Ms. Paxon disliked her so much, she felt a stab of anxiety every time she needed to pass the tiny cottage with one door and one window, Kaia remarked to Isadora that it was probably the lack of light and space that had made Ms. Paxon so angry.

Finally, there was also the little old lady who lived across the valley, she was tall and frail, slightly slouched with the purplest hair Kaia had ever seen, Kaia often thought that she was no more than a few stone and held upright by a beautiful walnut cane, her name was Elsa but Kaia always called her Ms. Elsa, she would bake apple tarts for Kaia on the occasional Saturday afternoons in the summertime, she knew Kaia went to Riverdale most weekends in the summertime and would call to talk and listen to Ms. Elsa's stories. Kaia always knew who she could trust in the Barony, mostly the older people; Kaia would daydream when they told her tales of their travels and adventures from their youth.

Kaia had excellent survival instincts from a young age. She loved exploring the area around where she lived. She used to spend hours running up and down the green rolling hills, and valleys too, the steep rolling valleys were covered in the most magnificent pine trees, and rock formations too, the rocks were so beautiful that Kaia would give each rock formation its own name, one particular rock was so high and dangerous and shaped like a seat, Kaia called this rock the giants throne, she sometimes wandered miles from home on her adventures. Nobody cared when she had gone from home for so long and nobody ever asked where she went to, which suited her just fine.

One day, when she was six years old, she had found a small fruit orchard. She lay in wait and watched for the farmer and learned his routine. Once she knew it was safe, she would climb the fence and help herself to some of the fruit that was being grown. Her eyes would light up like sunbeams when she would look into the orchard full of juicy fruits, ready for picking. She then used to munch on delicious juicy treats all the way back home. Pears were her favourite, but plums were so yummy too, Kaia always hoped that both fruits would be there when she visited. She was always careful to never be greedy and to only take enough to fill her belly. In nearly seven years, she had never told a soul other than Billow about the orchard – it was their secret.

She had happened upon Billow quite by accident during one of her outdoor adventures. She had wandered into

Riverdale, a dark forest and had been exploring between the trees when they had opened up into a clearing where the most majestic waterfall she had ever seen had catapulted down from a huge cliff with rainbows made of beautiful red, yellow, pink and orange cascading across the water at the base of the waterfall.. The water had been an electric blue and the grass surrounding the waterfalls pool had been the brightest emerald green. Even the rocks seemed to shimmer and shine. This little slice of heaven in the heart of the deep dark forest had seemed magical and she had quickly decided to spend the rest of the day here. She had been lying in the grass gazing at the vivid blue sky and listening to the water cascade down over the rocks when she had seen a movement out of the corner of her eye under one of the trees leading into the forest. Being more curious than a cat, Kaia had gone to investigate and she had discovered Billow. She froze for a instant while she considered what to do next. Impulsively she leaned forward to come face to face with Billow. He was a tiny handful of grey fluff with tinges of tiny white feathers which she had scooped up and held him firmly close to her chest. She suspected he was a dragon, but wasn't entirely sure as he was so small and fluffy with the biggest, widest eyes. She had thought he could maybe have been an owl. Her father was a dragon protector and he had a big laboratory that he spent most of his time in. It was stocked up with lots of books and pictures of dragons and on nights when she was too hungry to sleep she used to sneak inside and learn all she could about dragons. They were the most amazing creatures and they fascinated her, just as they did her father. It was the only thing that Kaia had in common with any member of her family.

She looked up into the tall trees and saw a huge nest balanced high up in the branches and knew at once that he had either fallen from the nest or had been rejected by his mother. Dragons, she knew, tended to push the runt of the litter from the nest almost as soon as they had been born so that all the food could go to the strongest baby dragons. Kaia didn't care if he was the runt, she thought he was beautiful. She had fallen in love with him as soon as she picked him up and had decided that he would be called Billow on the way home. Kaia had decided on his name quite by accident because the whole way home he had kept sneezing and burning her fingers with the tiny flames that billowed out of his nostrils.

"Hey if you keep burning me with those little plumes of fire that billow from your nose, I'm going to have to put you in a muzzle. I won't have any fingers left at this rate," she had affectionately told him while she rearranged her fingers for what felt like the thousandth time. He had looked up at her with his brilliant cyan eyes and given a loud purr like he understood what she had said.

"Hey that's it!" she had told him excitedly, "I'll call you Billow!" he had nuzzled himself into her neck and she knew that he approved of the name.

She had raced home and bolted through the door to her father's lab. She was so excited she didn't even stop to think how much trouble she might be in for disturbing his work. Her father was also an inventor and he was determined to invent a flying machine. His one true love was dragons and all of his spare time was taken taking care of or protecting them. His greatest wish was to be able to soar in the sky alongside one of his beloved dragons. This unfortunately meant that the local people thought he was a bit mad, but whenever one of them questioned him, he simply replied, "you just wait and see."

"Kaia!" her father bellowed, "You know I hate to be disturbed when I'm working."

"I know Papa," she replied, "but look what I found. Can I keep him, please?" She opened her hands and held the grey ball of fluff out for her father to inspect. He came closer and pushed his glasses further up the bridge of his nose so he could see properly.

"Is that a..." he began.

"Yes, it's a baby dragon," Kaia interrupted, unable to contain her excitement a minute longer.

"Well blow me over with a feather," he exclaimed and grinned at Kaia. "What a rare find. You are very lucky to have found one so young that you can hand rear," he had told her, "Often they are found when they are much bigger and they can be rather hard to tame. But when you find them so young, they are totally trainable and can be awesome companions."

It was a rare moment of bonding that Kaia remembered having with her father but it had only lasted a few minutes before he was back to his usual grumpy self.

"Please Papa," Kaia had begged, "I never ask for anything. Please may I keep him?"

He had looked at her long and hard before replying, "as long as you take care of it. I don't have time for anything but my flying machine at the moment and your mother has enough to deal with looking after the lot of you."

"Yes Papa," Kaia had told him, "I promise. He will be my responsibility."

She had skipped out of the lab and into the garden to show Isadora. She was the only one who would be happy for her anyway. Her brothers and sisters wouldn't care. That had been the start of an amazing friendship and to this day she couldn't imagine her life without Billow. He had certainly grown since then and had turned a brilliant white colour, but she knew he still had a lot more growing to do as she was still able to pick him up and carry him. Dragons lived for hundreds of years and grew quite slowly, so although he was seven in human years, he was still very much a baby. The previous month his wings had started to bud and he now had a short tail but he was still covered in soft white feathers. The two of them were inseparable and her happiest memory was of the day she found him. In fact it was the only truly happy memory she had of her childhood.

"So Billow," Kaia asked her dragon with a serious face. "You think you can aim a fireball sneeze at the dress and help a girl out?"

Billow looked up at her and gave a little snort that saw some silver smoke bubble out his nostrils.

"Yeah you're right. That would probably just get me into more trouble with mother, but I have to say a beating might be worth it just to get out of wearing that orange and brown monstrosity!"

Chapter 5

Kaia often wondered why her mother had bothered to have so many children because she didn't seem to like any of them, Kaia often said that Endor had no favourites, she didn't like any of them. For some reason Endor used the worst of her hatred solely for Kaia and she couldn't understand why. She did as much housework as the others, minded her manners well enough and held her tongue, as much as she could, but no matter how good she seemed to be it was never enough. Sometime around her eighth birthday she had stopped trying. She had realized she was never going to please her family and now she simply did what made her happy. If she got a beating for it, well then so be it.

If she was honest, she was mischievous and generally ended up causing mayhem without even trying. But there were also the times when she knew what she was doing was naughty but she did it anyway. In the beginning, she had really tried hard to make her mother happy and do the right thing, but no matter how hard she tried, she failed.

"If I am going to get in trouble for everything then I might as well do the things I am being accused of" Kaia often whispered to Billow when they would be heading off in yet another adventure. Kaia just couldn't seem to shake the feeling that her mother just fundamentally disliked her. That had been a hard fact to live with, but Isadora had always filled the void. It was Isadora who dried her tears when she was sad or hurt. It was Isadora who cared for her when she was sick and it was Isadora who made her realize her own worth as a person – after eight years.

Isadora had always told Kaia that it wasn't her fault, that you couldn't please everyone, that Endor was sickly and that when you felt so poorly all the time, it was bound to make you grumpy. Kaia agreed that while all that was undoubtedly true, this was her mother – surely the usual rules didn't apply. Surely your mother should love you no matter what? Kaia knew deep down that Isadora was trying to make her feel better and so she always responded to her platitudes with a happy smile and skipped off to play. But it had bugged Kaia because it just didn't make any sense. Kaia got regular beatings and seemed to make Endor reach a state of explosive rage simply by breathing the same air. Endor would be fast asleep and Kaia would tiptoe past her room on the way down the stairs and without fail every single time, Endor would wake up roaring at her for being disturbed. The others could thunder past her room shouting and stomp their way down the stairs and it never seemed to wake her. It was like Endor sensed when Kaia was near and it sent her into an instant state of irritation.

As a result Kaia tried her level best not to be in the house much at all. When Kaia wasn't out exploring the hills and valleys, she spent most of her time down at Isadora's cottage. She couldn't explain it, but she always felt so safe there. Tucked away behind the wall, it was easy to pretend that this was her life and Isadora was her mother and that the two of them were happy alone. When they were there together, there was lots of laughing, joking and even singing and dancing. They used to make up funny songs and actions and had a running competition to see who could be the goofiest. It was the place where Kaia didn't have to pretend. It was somewhere she could be entirely herself. If she was angry and she made something strange happen, she didn't have to worry because more often than not in Isadora's cottage it was something funny. One time she had stomped her foot so hard shouting about something Endor had done to her that the whole cottage began to shiver and shake and then it had started to giggle, like it was being tickled. That had been enough for Isadora and her to dissolve into laughter and the bad mood was instantly forgotten. When she got angry in the family home, it regularly ended up in something being broken or set alight. She had often asked Isadora about these strange happenings and Isadora had simply passed it off by saying, "when you are here, even when you are angry, your soul is happy and that's why you think you make funny things happen. But when you are there, your soul is unhappy and you think ugly thoughts. Perception is everything my dear."

And that was all Isadora would ever say on the subject which didn't give Kaia any more idea about why it was happening. Kaia had often caught her siblings spying on her when she was down at Isadora's cottage. They always pushed an empty barrel over to the wall surrounding the cottage and hoisted themselves up so they could peek over the top. Although Kaia pretended she didn't see them, she always knew they were there and it just made her and Isadora up the level of fun they were having. Kaia knew it drove her siblings and mother crazy to know that despite their best efforts she was still capable of having fun and being happy. Kaia chatted to Isadora about it the one day and asked, "Why does it bother them so much to see me having fun and enjoying myself? What's it to them?"

"Ah child, they are just jealous because they have such blackness in their hearts," Isadora had replied.

From that day onwards, Kaia had called the wall that surrounded Isadora's cottage "The Jealous Wall" and it had become a great source of entertainment for the two of them during their shenanigans in the cottage and generally ended in one of them whispering to the other in a funny voice. "Incoming, incoming, Jealous Wall to the left" or

"Jealous Wall, 2 'o clock" and caused the two of them to collapse in fits of giggles.

Kaia often thought that maybe six kids could take their toll on a person, but Endor seldom did anything to care for any of them and didn't seem to enjoy being in their company, so nobody was more puzzled than Kaia when she started noticing that Endor's belly was getting more and more swollen. At first she thought it was just because she spent all day in bed and didn't get any exercise, but then she realized what was happening and asked Isadora, who confirmed that Endor was expecting another baby. Kaia had vowed to protect this baby from Endor's wrath and be the best big sister in the world. She would be everything to the baby, everything that she had hoped she would get from her older siblings but hadn't. She would make sure that this baby got a shot at being happy.

She spent endless hours at her waterfall caught up in elaborate daydreams about finally having a human friend, a true sibling – the two of them and Billow were going to be inseparable. Kaia was going to bring the baby everywhere with her, to visit Elsa, to climb trees and explore the valleys. Kaia was brought back to reality by a gush of warm air which had come across the garden bringing with it the scent of lilies and roses from across the garden. She made a mental list of the adventures they would take together.

But Kaia should have known better. When the baby was born, Endor wouldn't allow her anywhere near him. She remembered offering to rock him to sleep the one day and how upset her mother had become.

"Allow you near Henry? She said, with her fists firmly clenched. What so he can turn into the same kind of filthy horrible little imp that you are? You are to stay away from him. Do you hear me?" she had cried at Kaia. She had tried to assure her mother that she was only trying to help her, but Endor was having none of it.

"If I see your grubby paws on this baby I will give you the beating of your life and lock you away in the attic and throw away the key," she had threatened.

"Mama, all I said is that I… I wanted to help you with the baby, that's all," Kaia objected, as she usually did but it fell on deaf ears. Kaia grimaced as a blow rained down on her shoulder from Endor's wafer thin sally rod, it was Endor's favourite punishment of choice when it came to Kaia, it sounded like a whip as it glided through the air, and she ran before another could make contact with her.

"Get up into that attic now Kaia," Endor growled in a tone much like that of a troll, "and this time you can stay there for the night, no supper and to ensure you do no sneak out I am going to lock the attic door". Kaia felt her tummy churn as she heard the keys rattling in Endor's hand, the sound of the heavy keys rattling of each other made her skin shudder with fear; Kaia was pushed up the stairs in from of Endor.

"Get in there you repulsive little imp, I do not want to hear a word from you for the rest of the night, I will be spending time with the Dennis and Henry" Endor whispered, with a smile that Kaia was not able to distinguish if it was a twisted smile or a sneer, it a happened so fast. Kaia sat on her bed thinking of what had she done so wrong to deserve being this life, how the children in the house next door had a mama and papa who loved them, hugged them, held their hands and played family games, there were no family games for Kaia, just fear and hurt.

That had been one of the worst days of Kaia's life. All the hopes and dreams she had of making her own little family within the one that despised her were shattered. She remembered running out the house with tears streaming down her face. Kaia hated crying but she couldn't help it. She had honestly thought her heart was going to break after the fight with her mother. Isadora had tried to stop her as she charged out of the house but she had shrugged her off and headed out into the garden to sit down by her favourite tree. She always felt so stifled inside the house, but the fresh air outside always seemed to calm her down. As she sat picking out tufts of grass and thinking about all that had been said, she realized that she was fighting a losing battle and that she had to harden her heart against her mother if she was going to survive the years until she was old enough to make it on her own.

She sat now out in the garden with Billow sleeping on the grass next to her, the sun warming her face and thought about that day with a wry smile. As it turned out, Henry wouldn't have been worth the effort. He was an absolute terror and had made her life that much worse since he had been born. In addition to getting into trouble for all she did wrong, she now took the blame for all he did wrong too. He used to bite her, pull her long hair and steal her bread. He hid her clean clothes out in the garden so they got dirty again and he followed her around teasing and taunting her until she lost her temper and caused something to shatter or break. He seemed to enjoy the fighting that followed her doing something unexplainable. The last incident had been especially hard to talk her way out of and since then Henry followed her around and whispered "witch!" under his breath.

It had all began on a quiet Sunday morning about a month ago. Breakfast was finished and Kaia was trying to clear the kitchen, but Henry thought it would be hilarious to throw the scraps of food all over the place. As she was scurrying this way and that, trying to contain the damage, he had grabbed the pepper shaker, opened it and thrown a whole handful of pepper into her face as she had turned around. Well she had sneezed so hard that she had turned every single grain of pepper into a flower with the sharpest, thorniest stems she had ever seen. The kitchen was full of them and Henry had gotten horribly pricked. For a moment nobody moved, and then Henry ran screaming from the kitchen. Thankfully it had just been her and Isadora left in the kitchen otherwise she would have found herself in very hot water. Isadora had helped her to clean up the mess and had expertly dodged her questions as to how what she had just seen happen was even possible.

"But Isadora," Kaia had begun. "Why do these things keep happening to me?"

"I've told you," Isadora said with an exasperated sigh. "I have no idea."

"But you must have some idea," Kaia had persisted. Isadora rolled her eyes in exasperation, "child how many times do I have to tell you the same thing?" "All I know is that you had better hope he doesn't disturb Endor or Iosaf with the flower story or your hide will be raw for days.

Now help me with these dishes!" And that had been her way of ending the conversation. Luckily for Kaia, when Henry had run with the story to Endor, it had been so unbelievable that she had thought he had been telling lies and he had been sent to his room with a warm ear. That had only made his anger for Kaia worse and he had started calling her a witch the very next day.

The very next morning Kaia decided that she wouldn't dwell on yesterday's strange events and she would go to the hazelnut tree in the valley below Riverdale called Edgeworth, it was a lovely autumn morning and the nuts were ready to pick, she loved roaming down to the giants chair, the name she gave the valley beyond Riverdale, especially when Billow would hop from stone to stone, she pretended he was playing hopscotch. After climbing to the top of the biggest hazelnut tree she could find Kaia gathered pockets full of nuts, Billow was not yet able to climb trees or fly up into them so he stood at the bottom of the tree staring incessantly up at Kaia, every few minutes he would circle the base of the tree to get a better look at where she was gone, now, Billow had the most acute hearing, he could hear an unfamiliar creaking in the tree, he stood bolt upright, head back with his mouth open, Kaia laughed at him as he looked like a dog, a very big dog. "What are you doing you silly dragon," she said stepping back to get a better look, she could hear a loud creek under her feet, the branch broke under her causing her to tumble head over heels, hitting branches and leaves on the way down, she flinched as branches and leaves hit her in the face, she was tumbling in mid-air for what seems like ages, she extended her arm out to grasp for any branches but it just hurt more so she retreated her arms back as close to her body as she could, "this is going to hurt," she thought to herself as she could see the ground coming to meet her, one last bough met her square in the chest winding her, she hit the ground with a thud, like a bag of sand.

Kaia lay still with her eyes closed for a few moments, trying to catch her winded breath, as it became a little easier to breath Kaia slowly opened her eyes and looked around her, staring at her like a puppy was Billow, breathing into her face, mouth open with a concerned look on his face. "Hi Billow, I think I will lay here for a little while if you don't mind," she said in a shallow breath, still not able to breathe deeply. Billow nodded back to her as if he had completely understood every word she had said. Kaia slowly moved one arm, then the other, then one leg and then the other, she could move everything and it didn't hurt much either, she sat up and felt a little dizzy. She sat upright for a little while waiting for the dizziness to ease before she tried to stand up. Like a baby learning to walk Kaia took little steps to start with, as she stood taller and taller without pain she knew how lucky she just had been. Pausing, she stood looking up at the tree which was branch and leafless all along one side where Kaia had knocked those off on her way down. She realised how lucky she had been.

Kaia made her way home, hobbling slightly, a limp on her right side made the journey arduous and hard. She knew that she could not tell her family what had happened, she knew they would not believe her nor care either. After arriving home she realised that no one was home so worrying about telling the family what happened didn't matter anymore. She looked around the house and there was no one, it was a little scary if she was honest, she had rarely seen the house empty, she felt a little lonesome, but that wasn't to last long. Kaia decided to clean up and go to bed, she was still sore after all, just as she had finished mopping the kitchen floor, Henry bounded onto the freshly washed slate floor leaving long mucky boot prints where she had slid from one end to the other, "Henry, stop that, I've just finished mopping that floor,", Henry taunted her by stomping his boots down hard on the floor, "Henry" Screeched Kaia, "get out," with that Endor came in and looked at the mess that met her in the kitchen. "Kaia, what in the world have to done to my floor, and trying to trip Henry up too, you are an evil child?" Endor looked at Kaia with a face like thunder and shouted. "Go to you room you imp, I cannot stand to look at you for one more second."

Kaia felt empty as she walked up to her bedroom, she walked in and closed the door, she took a deep breath and sighed, "is this it, is this my life?" as she turned and pressed her back against the door, she knew she didn't have to lock as no one would be coming to check on her, they never did. As Kaia sat thinking about things, she was sure she

63

would see the amusing side of all of this one day. She imagined that the only reason she managed to keep up hope of some kind of a happy future was because of Isadora and Billow and that was fine with her. They were her life line in this horrid family and they kept her sane.

She looked over at the still sleeping Billow, then leaned back on her elbows and tilted her face up, she closed her eyes and savoured the warm sun and took a deep breath. Spring was her favourite season when all the flowers bloomed – the air always smelled so clean and fragrant. As she lay relaxing she heard a rustling noise in the bushes that ran between her house and the next door neighbours.

 "Dennis!" she thought, sitting up quickly. He was her nemesis! She firmly believed he was put on this earth to torment her – as if her life wasn't difficult enough!

As she sat up she looked up and saw a big clump of mud come sailing over the bushes. It missed her by a hair. "Really?" she thought. "At almost thirteen years old, this is what amuses your simple mind?" As Kaia turned back around to Billow she muttered under her breath "horrid boy! Horrid, horrid boy.

She moved over, nudged Billow awake and looked up just in time to see a frog sailing through the air. Kaia got cross. Mud was one thing, but she couldn't stand it when people hurt innocent animals. Dennis had terrorized her for most of her childhood. He had pinched her, thrown mud at her, sent rocks shooting at her out of his catapult, drenched her with water in the dead of winter so she caught her death of cold, he had called her names and even cut all her hair off when she was five years old.

He had been very nervous of her once she had found Billow however, because he was such a coward. Every time Billow had sneezed and blown out a small flame his face had gone white and he had always run home to hide behind his mother's skirts. For the last few years he had run more covert operations of terror like today, sending mud and frogs flying at her because he was scared to get too close to her dragon. The truly funny part was that Kaia wasn't like most girls, she had always been a bit of a tomboy and in fact quite liked frogs and didn't mind being dirty because it was an excuse to go to her waterfall for a swim. What bugged Kaia was the terrified look in the poor frog's eyes as he soared high above the ground and Kaia felt a fresh surge of anger.

Kaia positioned herself carefully to catch the poor frightened frog and when he landed gently in her out stretched hands instead of splatting onto the floor, Kaia could have sworn he let out a huge sigh of relief. She set him down gently on the ground once she had made sure he wasn't hurt and watched him hop off into the long grass at the bottom of the garden near Isadora's cottage.

"Yes, that's much safer," Kaia whispered, "But now, what to do about that awful dragon turd next door!"
Billow gave an indignant huff and a puff of smoke shot out his nostrils signalling his displeasure.
"Yeah, you're right Billow," Kaia said ruffling his feathers, "Even your turds are better than that slug."
Kaia looked around for something to exact her revenge on Dennis and when she saw nothing, she got even more

cross and clenched her fists tightly at her sides. She stomped her foot and looked up at the sky in irritation. "Arrrrgh!" she shouted.

She heard Dennis giggle from behind the bushes and got even more cross because she knew he thought she was screaming because of the frog and the mud when that wasn't the real reason at all. As she stomped again at how unfair it all was, she heard a cawing noise in the tree above her and looked up to see a raven of the inkiest black she had ever seen. He gave an almighty caw before he took off from the branch, gained speed, then tucked his wings back and went into a dive.

Kaia's mouth fell open in disbelief – the raven was heading straight for the bushes where Dennis was hidden. Billow's eyes were also wide as the two of them stood frozen, watching. The next minute they heard Dennis screaming and crying, "Help! Help! MAMMY HELP ME!!!! This crazy bird is pecking me!"

Kaia couldn't help herself. She ran over to the bushes and peered through and clutched her sides as she laughed, watching Dennis run around his garden with the raven in hot pursuit pecking at his arms, legs and ears.

"Serves him right!" Kaia said to Billow, "I hope that taught him a lesson about being kinder to animals!"

Billow gave a snort.

"Yeah, you're right. Probably not."

Chapter 6

It was the night before Kaia's thirteenth birthday and Isadora was in a state! She was jumpy and fidgety and kept dropping things from excitement

"Isadora!" screeched Endor, "Can you get yourself together. Just now you are going to break something."

"Yes ma'am, sorry ma'am," Isadora muttered apologetically as she picked up a spoon she had dropped.

"All this noise is not good for my frayed nerves," Endor continued. "I have just got up out of bed and now you are giving me a headache. Iosaf has insisted I join the family for dinner to keep my strength up and now you're trying to drive me back to bed!"

Isadora turned her back to the table and rolled her eyes. Endor's dramatics were starting to get a bit much, especially in her nervous state. It wasn't like she was dropping stuff on purpose but she kept expecting a huge portal to suddenly open in the middle of the kitchen and then she would have some explaining to do.

She laid out the plates for dinner and started setting the bowls of food out on the table. As usual Kaia had been banished to her attic room for turning a spool of thread into a rat that had bitten her brother Tom on the thumb. Naturally, the family didn't know she had actually turned the thread into the rat – they just thought she had the rat in her pocket and had set him loose to attack Tom when he had been trying to stab her hand with a fork at the table.

"Can you not take a joke Kaia?" Endor had shouted, one side of her mouth curling into a grimace, "Tom is just playing a game with you."

Kaia as usual had been unable to hold her tongue and had shouted back at her mother, "he is trying to stab me with a fork!!!" But her protests had fallen on deaf ears and shouting at her mother had sealed her fate.

"Get to your room," Endor screamed, "and I don't want to see you dirty face for the rest of the night, you horrid creature!"

Kaia had pushed her chair out from the table with so much force that it had fallen over and she had stomped her way out of the kitchen and up the stairs. The whole house shook as she slammed the attic trap door behind her.

"She is SO lucky I am feeling so weak tonight," Endor had stated, "Otherwise I would march up there and give her a hiding she wouldn't forget in a hurry. Slamming doors, setting vermin on the other children. That girl has no respect and no manners!"

"Respect is earned my dear," Isadora said quietly to herself. Isadora knew that Endor had to maintain her reputation within the family as the feared matriarch and that was the reason for her little speech, but Endor knew deep down that Kaia was long past taking her beatings lying down and that if she tried to hit her now that she was a teenager, Kaia would fight to defend herself. Kaia had grown into a strong girl, both mentally and physically. She still had a slight build from being malnourished, but her arms and legs were

71

muscular from all the running and climbing she did when she went off on her adventures. She was also very tall and was almost the same height as Endor now. One of the standing jokes within the family was to call Kaia a giraffe and make fun of her for her height. She was the only tall one amongst the nine of them but only Isadora knew that being tall was a trait from her real family, the family Isadora hoped Kaia would get to meet the following day.

Isadora busied herself at the sink while Iosaf and Endor tucked into their dinner. It was a rare night where Henry, Tom and Edith had joined Endor and Iosaf at the table. They were rarely allowed any of Iasof's meat, but had each been given a chunk of fresh bread with some hot gravy and a couple of potatoes. Isadora had carefully hidden a bit of meat with some fresh bread in one of her dishcloths to take and give to Kaia later – it was after all a very special birthday. She tucked the dish cloth into the pocket of her apron and silently exited the kitchen. She needn't have worried, the rest of them were so busy eating they didn't really take much notice of what she was doing anyway.

Isadora made her way to the attic and knocked gently on the trap door four times. It was a signal they had agreed on years ago. However, Isadora was the only person who ever knocked anyway. Usually if someone needed her they just barged in without the courtesy of knocking. Generally though, nobody bothered her when she was in the attic – out of sight, out of mind. But the little knocking tradition with them had stuck anyway because that's what real families did and Isadora was Kaia's only real family.

Kaia opened the trap door and looked into Isadora's kind eyes.

"Here child, take this quickly," Isadora whispered as she shoved the rolled up dishcloth with the 'food inside into Kaia's hands.

"Thank you," Kaia began.

"No time for that now, I have to get back before they realize I'm gone. Kaia, tomorrow is a very important day. Please don't go wandering off like you usually do. Try to stay close to home." Isadora asked.

"Why?"

"Kaia," Isadora said in a weary tone, "Can you never just do as you are asked?"

"Okay," Kaia replied out loud, but under her breath she added, "fat chance!"

Kaia was getting tired of the riddles and the strange requests that she didn't understand the reasons for. She wasn't a child anymore and she knew when someone wasn't being entirely honest with her. She just wished Isadora would come out and tell her what was going on. Kaia knew that Isadora had her best interests at heart but she was in a defiant mood on the eve of her birthday. She had a plan and as Isadora had said, it was HER day. Surely she could spend it how she wished. And all she wanted to do was escape to the waterfall and spend her day with Billow being happy and carefree.

Isadora gave her a stern glare and Kaia said while crossing her fingers behind her back, "I promise Isadora, I won't go far."

"Right, I'll be off then. Goodnight Kaia, sleep well," Isadora said with a tired smile, "See you in the morning."

Kaia shut the trap door and went back to her plans. She had been carefully wrapping up some decent clothes in a blanket and tying it together with a long piece of string when Isadora interrupted her. She speedily unwrapped the clothes parcel and added the food to her things and wrapped it up again, tying it together tightly. She left a long piece of string hanging on the end and pushed the parcel under her bed.

She climbed into bed and looked over at the window where the dreadful orange and brown dress hung. The mere sight of that horrid dress made Kaia's stomach churn, but she knew after tomorrow she would never have to wear it again. "Humpf," she thought and then smiled. "They think they can still force me to do things. Well I'll show them!"

Kaia sucked in a quick breath and ran her plans for tomorrow through her head one last time, happy in the thought that she was going to get one up on her awful family and on her birthday no less, she nodded off into a peaceful slumber.

***

Isadora felt exhausted. She had finished all her work in the house and was in her cottage for the night. She sat on her rocking chair and tried to calm down, but she just couldn't settle. Not even her usual lavender infused tea had helped to soothe and quiet her mind. Her shoulders tightened as she nervously thought about tomorrow.

Her first fear was that she would miss the portal. She didn't know for sure where it was going to appear, but she assumed it would be in the kitchen, the same place it had dropped her twelve years before. She didn't know how long it would stay open for or what would happen if she missed it. She hoped that when the passage was no longer locked that Catherine would have some way of finding her and taking Kaia back to Cypathia, but she didn't know how as Catherine had no idea where she had ended up. She was so frustrated because all this portal-making business had been new to both her and Catherine so she really wasn't sure about anything. She also had received no word in twelve years of what had happened in the battle.

Was there even a home to go back to? Had Kaia's parents survived? Were they going to be going home for Kaia to ascend the throne as Queen or would they be walking into a kingdom run by King Mordor, who would surely execute her for treason or at the very least lock them up in a dungeon for the rest of their life. She also worried that even if everything worked out perfectly and the portal appeared as it should, would she have the ability to transport herself and Kaia back to the right place after messing up so badly and landing them in Herecia in the first place, Isadora became tense and felt a tightness in her forehead, it felt like it hurt to think..

And Kaia, she was going to be so angry when she found out. Isadora wrung her hands together anxiously. She dreaded telling Kaia the truth, most especially because she knew that Kaia already suspected that she wasn't being entirely honest. She was so worried that Kaia would turn on her when she came clean. Isadora was the only person that Kaia trusted in the world and she was scared that she might not be able to handle another betrayal. She just hoped that Kaia would sit and listen to her story and keep an open mind. She hadn't meant to cause any harm and she lived every day with the guilt of landing Kaia in the middle of such a horrid "family" that had made her life so awful. She loved Kaia like a daughter and had never wanted her to be hurt so badly. It was little comfort that despite it all, Kaia had grown into a strong young girl who took most things in her stride.

Isadora stood up and stretched her aching body. She walked over to the window and debated performing some magic to try leading her to the portal, but she was terrified that she would end up hiding it away instead. Isadora was so insecure in her magical ability away from Catherine's guidance that she had only ever used magic when it was absolutely unavoidable since their arrival and she had always stuck to spells she knew really well. Her experiments usually tended to not go as planned, so despite wanting to turn Endor into a warty old toad many times over the years, she had managed to keep control. Isadora had always remembered Catherine's wise words and used to repeat them like a mantra when the urge took her to zap someone into a cockroach. Catherine had always placed her hands on Isadora's shoulders and whispered *"Patience young one. All good things come to those who wait. Bide your time and what you seek will come to you."* She just hoped that she would have a chance to get her revenge on the monsters that had made Kaia's life so difficult.

She gave a loud sigh as she looked up at the starry sky. It was gone midnight and officially Kaia's birthday. She hated sitting around doing nothing and feeling so helpless, but there was nothing else she could do but wait. She decided to trust that the portal would be drawn to her magical aura and make its presence known to her at the right time.

"Right," she said aloud to the deep dark night, "I need to get some rest now. Tomorrow is a big day and I need to be ready." She crossed the floor to her bed, pulled back the covers, climbed inside and fell into a fitful, restless sleep.

Chapter 7

Kaia's birthday dawned clear and bright. She stretched out in bed and looked out her tiny attic window and watched the sun rise up over the horizon and she knew that nothing was going to ruin her day. She sat up and nudged Billow who was still snoring at the foot of her bed. Thin wisps of silvery smoke floated out of his nostrils every time he exhaled and Kaia's heart filled with love.

"Wake up you lazy dragon," she told him as she stroked him awake, "today is my birthday!"

He opened one eye and rolled over onto his back so Kaia could scratch his tummy. This was the routine every morning. If Kaia didn't scratch his tummy, he was in a bad mood for the rest of the day. Once she was done, she hopped out of bed and slipped the orange and brown dress on over her head. It was too small for her tall frame so in addition to being hideously ugly, it was also uncomfortable and she felt trapped in it like her arms being tied down by her side.

Billow looked at her and grunted. "I know, I know," Kaia told him, "I look dreadful. But don't worry it's not for long. I've got a plan."

She reached under her bed and pulled out the parcel of clothes and food she had wrapped up the night before. She pushed open the small window and holding tightly onto the long end of rope, she pushed the parcel out the window and gently lowered it to the ground. She was very lucky because her room was at the back of the house and looked down on the bushes that surrounded the property. The parcel landed on the ground and was hidden from view by the wild bush that grew there.

"Phase one, complete," Kaia said to Billow with a wink, "Come on down to breakfast for phase two." Kaia made her bed, and fluffed up her pillows like she did every day, she brushed her hair back into a ponytail, she normally had a fishtail plait but she thought she would have a change for today. She looked around her room, "it looks smaller than usual, maybe it is because I'm getting bigger but this room looks narrower than before" she thought to herself closing the door behind her. Billow wouldn't budge from outside the bedroom door, he just stood there staring at Kaia, he tilted his head ever so slightly to the right, then he straightened it back up and stared at her again, Kaia was feeling a little uncomfortable at his behaviour, "Billow, move, this instant, you are scaring me acting like this," Billow looked at her and started walking towards the landing, briefly halting momentarily to look at Kaia. She felt that he knew it was her birthday and was being extra attentive to her, a dragons was of saying happy birthday "Come on you silly dragon, let's get downstairs and get breakfast and get this big day underway"

The two of them made their way down the passage and predictably as soon as she got to the top of the stairs outside her mother's room, she heard Endor stirring and braced herself for the shouting.

"KAIA!!!" came an angry voice seconds later. "Is that you and that dragon of yours making all that racket and waking me up?"

"Right on time," Kaia whispered to Billow.

In a louder voice she added, "yes mother, it's me. I'm so sorry to have disturbed you." As she had expected, her polite answer brought her mother out of the room immediately.

"What are you up to?" Endor began, and then stopped dead in her tracks at the sight of Kaia in the dress. Endor narrowed her eyes at Kaia. "Why are you wearing that dress? I thought you hated it?"

Kaia plastered a sweet smile on her face and replied, "mother, I thought about what you said and I realized you were right. I was being ungrateful. Since today is my thirteenth birthday, I decided it was time to turn over a new leaf. I decided to wear the dress. Don't you think it looks lovely?"

Endor stood and gawked at Kaia, completely unsure how to respond. She could not, simply would not, give her a compliment. Besides it would be a huge lie to say that. They stood that way for a minute or so, before Endor, clearly beaten, turned on her heel and headed back to bed. "Just get out of my sight before you ruin my day," she snapped at Kaia before slamming her door shut.

Kaia stifled a giggle. "Not even a 'happy birthday' for her youngest daughter. What a surprise," she said as she and Billow headed down the stairs. They passed by the door of the kitchen and saw Isadora emptying out all the cupboards and peering deeply inside. Kaia raised an eyebrow at Billow. She looked like a crazy person with half her body disappeared inside the cupboard.

Curiosity got the better of Kaia and she just had to know. "What on earth are you doing Isadora?" Kaia asked, "Are you looking for something?"

Isadora got such a fright that she banged her head on the cupboard as she straightened up and turned around. "What... Oh, it's you Kaia dear," Isadora said rubbing the bump on her head.

"No I'm just cleaning. I thought I saw a family of spiders had made their home inside there, but now I can't seem to find them," Isadora told her.

Kaia looked at Isadora, her eyebrows meeting in suspicion, but didn't say anything more about it. "Ok, well I'm off to the waterfall today. I'll see you later."

"Kaia," Isadora called after her, "Wait a moment."

Kaia stopped and turned to face Isadora who enveloped her in a great big hug in the door way of the kitchen. "Happy birthday, darling child," she said, "Enjoy your day and don't be home too late."

"Thank you Isadora, I won't," she promised.

And with that she skipped happily out the door with Billow contently following behind. As soon as they were outside, Kaia turned to Billow. "Quick, this way," Billow was puffing hard, and struggling to keep up with Kaia; his legs were short so they moved in double time. "Billow you look so funny when you run after me," Kaia giggled as she ran. But he was adamant and kept up with the pace.

She led Billow around the back of the house and crawled under the bushes to retrieve her parcel. She quickly pulled off the horrible orange and brown dress and slipped on her favourite comfortable clothes. She wrapped the dress up in the parcel and tossed it back under the bush. She grabbed the food parcel. "Right, now I'm ready for the day. Let's get out of here before someone sees us."

The two of them ran as fast as they could to the bottom of the garden, they jumped over the gate and disappeared off into the distance.

***

Kaia sat in the lush grass looking at the beautiful aquamarine water fall over the rocks. She was eating a juicy orange and her chin was covered in sticky sweet citrus juice. She and Billow had taken the path past the orchard so they could get some fresh fruit for a birthday picnic and the two of them had feasted happily on their spoils. Kaia had shared her meat from Isadora with Billow and he had nuzzled her neck appreciatively afterwards. She knew Billow was forced to hunt because he wasn't given any decent meat. Dragons loved chicken, but Iosaf certainly wasn't going to waste his precious meat on Kaia's pet. So poor Billow was forced to eat rats and bugs. She knew how much the rare treat she had shared with him had meant to him.

"Wow! I'm so sticky," Kaia exclaimed. "That fruit was so juicy and delicious. I'm going to swim now and clean up." Kaia usually went for a long swim after a feast of juicy fruit, the water looked amazing glistening like a silvery mirror on top of the water, and the waterfall hit the water with such grace that it hardly made any splash when it entered. Kaia thought it was magical looking; she never tired looking at its beauty.

Billow purred in answer. Kaia knew he didn't mind being left alone for a bit. His tummy was full and he would want to have a nap in the warm sun. Kaia gave him a kiss on his head as he settled down for his siesta and stood up and made her way down to the water's edge. Was it her imagination or did the water look especially clear and bright today?

87

"Maybe I'm just looking through more mature eyes now that I'm thirteen," she joked with herself. She didn't bother taking off her clothes. She knew she would dry in the warmth of the sun as she made her way home. She positioned herself on a big rock and dived into the cool water. Rays of red, orange and purple danced and mirrored up from the river bed with the most magnificent colours shining along the water edge.

"AAAAAAAAH! So refreshing," she thought as she came up for air and flipped herself over onto her back to float along in the pool at the base of the waterfall. She turned herself around so she was facing the water fall. It was such a relaxing place; she often wondered how come she had never fallen asleep watching the water crash down into the pool. She couldn't explain it and had no idea why she was so drawn to this place. It was truly her slice of heaven in an otherwise dreadfully dull and dreary world.

As she lay on her back floating along in the cool water something got her attention and struck her as strange. While the waterfall was usually very blue with crystal clear water, today something looked a little off. It was almost as if there was a bright light shining out from behind the curtain of water because today the water looked extra shimmery and glittery – almost magical.

She shook her head at herself. "Magical, could it truly be? There's no such thing as magic Kaia. You've been out in the sun too long" she said to herself, but she just couldn't shake the feeling that something was different about her waterfall today.

She fought the curiosity for as long as she could before she decided to go investigate. She had climbed the rocks behind the waterfall lots of times and she knew exactly where to put her feet so she wouldn't fall or get knocked down by the torrent of falling water. She pulled herself up onto the ledge and made her way carefully around in the space between the rocks on her left and the wall of water on her right. As she came around to where the water flow was strongest she stopped and her eyes widened in surprise.

"What on earth is that?" Kaia said out loud.

There in front of her, the normally dark brown rocks had changed to a silver colour and instead of looking like rocks it looked like a tall curtain except it was set inside where the rocks generally were. It wasn't very wide, just wide enough for someone to walk through – almost like a door, except there was no handle.

Kaia was puzzled. What could it be? Who put it here? She had never encountered anyone at her waterfall before and she had been coming here for years. She reached out a hand to touch it, but then quickly pulled it back. What if it hurt her? She had never seen anything like it before. After a quick argument in her head with herself, Kaia reached out her hand again to touch the silvery thing in the rocks.

For a second she was irritated with herself when she noticed her fingers were shaking because she had always thought of herself as brave, but then she comforted herself with the thought that this could be a very dumb idea – one that was potentially very dangerous – even for her!

Slowly…very slowly… she reached out her index finger and poked the silver wall. It felt soft and a bit squishy. "Mmmmm, that's so strange," Kaia thought.

She pulled her finger out. None of the substance was on her finger. She sniffed her finger but couldn't smell any odour at all. She put her hand palm up against the wall but didn't push her hand in this time. She just gently moved her palm back and forth to see what happened. The whole wall wobbled and shivered like jelly.

Finally curiosity got the better of her. "Oh what the heck," she said as she jammed her hand into the wall elbow deep. What a strange sensation. It was like she was being sucked inside. She couldn't see her hand and she couldn't see where the wall could possibly lead to. She quickly pulled her arm out and heard suction and a popping sound as she pulled her hand free.

By now Kaia's heart was hammering wildly in her chest and she knew that no matter how brave she thought she was, there was no ways she was going to just walk into some funny silvery substance to heavens knew where. She made her way back to the edge of the ledge and dived back into the pool. She swam the short distance to the other side of the pool and pulled herself up on the rocks.

There was only one thing she could think of to do. She ran to where Billow was snoozing on the grass, shook him awake and said, "come on Billow, we have to go fetch Isadora. She'll know what to do." Billow woke up and was completely perplexed by Kaia's behaviour, all this flapping and shuffling, if he had arms he would scratch his head. He decided just to follow Kaia wherever she was going, just like he always did.

After what seemed like hours running, but in fact was three or four minutes, Kaia stopped to take a breath, just for one minute to take in everything she had just seen - Then it struck her, there were shapes in the shimmering wobbling jelly, she was too preoccupied with her arm inside to look around, but now she could remember seeing the shapes" – "What were those shapes?" she said out loud to herself, "were they people?, they looked like people" she sat down and tried to relax her mind just enough to concentrate on what they shapes were but she was no able to keep her mind still, even for one second. "I... I am going back," she said to Billow, with a quiver in her voice, "I must go back and see what those shapes are." All kinds of thoughts were racing through her mind as she returned to the waterfall. As she approached the waterfall the curtain was still shimmering, and the rocks were still a silvery colour, Kaia walked quietly, she could feel herself tip toe to the rocks, "Stop it you silly girl, tip toe is hardly going to help," she thought to herself as she got closer.

When she came to the edge of the river she paused, took a deep breath and entered the water, she swam a little and stopped – "She could see the shimmering lights but no shapes, she decided to proceed slowly until she reached the edge of the curtain with the shimmering jelly, still no shapes, "maybe I was just imagining it, that's it, imagining, of course, but what if, if it is not my imagination, what if it only happens when I put my arm in," she murmured to herself with a tremble in her voice. With that she plunged her arm in, "no point playing about with a finger first," she thought. As she waved her arm about in the jelly she watched eagerly, her eyes darting over and back to try to catch a glimpse of the shapes she was so sure she had seen the last time. She stood completely still, listening intently but nothing.

As she removed her arm, her wrist bone started tingling and Kaia looked up and there it was the shapes she had seen the first time. She stood, unmoving, intent of figuring out what the shapes were, she called out gently "who are you, what is your name, what are you looking for?" she stood staring at the shapes to hear their voices but alas, nothing. A tingle of fear and excitement ran up her spine as she heard a mumbled and garbled voice speak to her, she could feel the shape touching the tips of her finger, she got pins and needles in her fingers where they had touched her hand. She pulled her hand out with lightning speed, afraid that they wold bite her hand off, she thought she was a little irrational but told herself she was doing the right thing as it was pretty irresponsible of her to put her hand in the jelly in the first place without knowing what was in there.

She looked intently at the shimmering jelly again to try to communicate but there she could not see anything, "I think I shall have to put my arm in again if I am going to find out who these shapes are" she said with a lump in her throat. She plunged her arm back into the shimmering jelly with conviction and waited, there was a pause… Kaia's eyes widened with excitement as she could see the shapes more clearly this time, they were very tall, not like giants as giants surely were tall but also wide, theses shapes well tall and so thin, they were like stretched humans, white and glowing, shimmering like the jelly only white not silvery. Kaia wondered how the wind didn't knock them over. "Who are you, or can I be so rude as to even ask, what are you?" Kaia nervously said in a loud whisper, Kaia patiently awaited the reply as she attentively waited for the answer "we are the keepers of the portal," came the reply, Kaia felt confused as she could hear them answer her but she could not see their mouths move, "I'm sorry but how can you talk if your mouth does not move," Kaia nervously and excitedly asked. "We communicate by telepathy" came the reply, Kaia knew that surely she had gone mad from all of the excitement and everything she had seen was an hallucination, she said thank you to the shapes and removed her arm, she hung her head, a little sad that she was indeed hallucinating, "I must go and get Isadora, I cannot wait any longer," she sighed - Kaia took a deep breath and ran as fast as she could back to Isadora's cottage to tell her about everything that had taken place at the waterfall and inform Isadora of her newly found realisation of her insanity.

Chapter 8

Kaia didn't think she had ever run so fast before, even Billow was having trouble keeping up with her. She hopped over the fence to her garden and was in such a hurry to get to Isadora she completely forgot to change back into her dress in case her mother saw her. She burst through the kitchen door, breathless and sweaty, "Isadora?" she panted to Henry who was sitting at the kitchen table. "Where's Isadora?"

"I dunno," he said with a sly grin.

Isadora crossed the kitchen and grabbed him by the ear, "listen here you little turd. Tell me where she is now, before I turn you into a spider and stomp on you!"

Henry's eyes grew wider as Kaia spoke and he stammered, "She isn't feeling well. Papa sent her to lie down in her cottage."

Kaia let him go and raced back across the kitchen. As she reached the door, she heard Henry mutter, "witch!" but she was in too much of a hurry. She would deal with him later.

As she had made her way home, her head had been filled with all kinds of ideas about what the silver wall could be. Was it a doorway to a magical place? Was it something that other people were going to use to come and attack them? Perhaps she had just imagined it? She knew better than anyone that she had a very active imagination. Her ideas had become wilder and wilder until she had thought she wouldn't be able to bear it anymore, so by the time she got to Henry, her nerves were rather frayed. She knew she would pay for hurting him later when Endor heard about it. And she had no doubt that he would run off to tell tales and get her into trouble. Getting Kaia into trouble had become Henry's hobby and he did it well.

She rounded the corner and ran past the Jealous Wall to the gate and nearly knocked Isadora right off her feet. "Good heavens child! Where have you been?" Isadora shouted, taking hold of Kaia by the shoulders.

"Isadora! You won't believe what I found. You have to come with me now and look," Kaia told her then seemed to realize that Isadora was outside, "Hang on a minute, aren't you supposed to be sick in bed?"

Kaia didn't think she had ever seen Isadora looking so wild and stressed before. Isadora remained her rock. She was always calm no matter what was going on so to see her so clearly freaked out made Kaia feel very uneasy. They both stared at one another in silence for a few seconds, neither one sure whether to speak, until finally Isadora seemed to sag with defeat. She took Kaia by the hand and led her inside. "Tell me what's got you so excited," she said.

"Well," Kaia began, "I went down to my waterfall with Billow today for my birthday and while I was swimming it was like the water was glowing. It was so bright and shiny and I just had to go and investigate." I wasn't sure if I should Isadora, her voice trembling with excitement and insecurity at the same time, but I did, I did you know, are you proud of me Isadora, are you, are you?

Isadora sighed, her blue eyes looking concerned yet intrigued; she sank back onto her rocking chair. She knew how Kaia could ramble on when she told her stories and this one seemed set to be a particularly long one. Isadora normally paid attention to what Kaia said, but today she was finding it rather difficult to concentrate on Kaia's chattering when she was fighting to keep the panic about the portal under control. She couldn't imagine why it hadn't appeared to her before now and she was starting to worry that something had gone wrong with the spell and they would be trapped in Herecia forever or worse yet that somehow the portal was standing open in some other realm that they would never be able to get to because she had messed up so badly twelve years ago.

Suddenly, Isadora sat bolt upright in her chair and nearly toppled over. "What did you just say?" she demanded of Kaia.

"Really Isadora, what the matter with you today?" Kaia asked, "Are you sure you're alright?"

"Yes, yes, I'm fine," Isadora said with a dismissive wave of her hand. "Tell me again slowly what you just said."

"I said," Kaia repeated with deliberate slowness, "that I found this big silver jelly-like curtain behind my waterfall and I put my arm inside the jelly and when I had my arm in there I could see shiny people," she said with one long breath "I asked who they were and they said they were the keepers of the portal, and Isadora I know I have finally gone mad because…"

Kaia stopped talking as Isadora burst into tears. Kaia watched her as the tears streamed down her face, but was so confused because at the same time as she was crying she was also smiling.

Isadora got herself together and went over to sit next to Kaia on the big sofa. She took her by the hand and looked kindly and pleadingly into her eyes. "My child, I have lots to tell you. Firstly, you are not insane. Finally I can tell you the truth about who you are. All I ask is that you hear me out and try to keep any anger you may feel towards me in check until you have heard the whole story."

Chapter 9

Kaia sat wide eyed with disbelief as Isadora told her the story of how they had ended up in Endor and Iosaf's home. By some kind of miracle, Kaia managed to keep quiet throughout. Finally, Isadora ended and asked, "so that's it, the whole truth. Are you very angry with me?"

Kaia looked at Isadora, really seeing her for the first time. This woman had risked her life to keep her safe from harm. This woman had been the only one to show her love or affection over. She couldn't be mad at her. Everything she had done had been for Kaia's benefit.

Finally when Isadora thought she was going to burst waiting for Kaia to say something, she said, "So you're telling me that I'm a princess from another kingdom who probably has some kind of magical powers and I had to escape as a baby to stop the Evil King from capturing me.

We now have to go through the jelly wall which is actually a portal to another place, so that I can ascend the throne and become the ruler of the kingdom that we ran away from?"

Isadora nodded her head. "Yes."

"But," Kaia continued, "that means that the people here, Endor and Iosaf and my brothers and sisters, they actually aren't my family at all?"

"No," Isadora agreed. "They are absolutely no relation to you at all. This is just where the portal spat us out after I got us lost."

Kaia jumped up and shouted as loud as she could, "WOOOOOOOHOOOOOOO!"

Isadora looked panicked again. She was worried that she had told Kaia too much at once and she was having some sort of breakdown from all the information. But as she watched Kaia, she realized she was happy and celebrating. Kaia grabbed Isadora by the hands pulling her to her feet and spun her around in a circle before pulling her into a hug. "Isadora, thank you. This is THE best birthday present EVER!"

Isadora hugged Kaia back, so relieved that Kaia hadn't been angry or decided to run away in one of her fits of temper like she normally did. They hugged each other, whooped, laughed and cried together before Kaia suddenly stopped, looked at Isadora and demanded, "Well, what are we waiting for? Let's get Billow and get out of here and go meet my real family. I'm so excited. I can't wait. I just know they are going to be so amazing. This explains everything. It was never my fault – I'm not the black sheep of the family after all."
Isadora giggled. Kaia's enthusiasm was infectious.

They were both so caught up in the happiness of the moment that neither of them noticed a pair of beady, sly eyes peering over the Jealous Wall overhearing every word of Isadora's story. As the celebrations continued in the cottage, the person slid quietly down the wall, sloped across the garden and swiftly let themselves into the kitchen of the main house.

As Kaia and Isadora sat and made their final arrangements and Isadora told Kaia a little more about her past, they heard a strange noise outside Isadora's cottage. They gave each other a look and Isadora put her finger to her lips indicating that Kaia should be quiet. With one hand on her amulet, she made her way outside to see what had made the noise. Kais followed close behind listening carefully. They rounded the side of the cottage and got the fright of their lives.

Kaia screamed and tried to run but something hit her over the head. She felt hands grab her wrists and in the scuffle she heard Isadora cry out, "no!. Unhand me you vermin!"

Kaia was seeing stars from the blow to her head, but she fought against her attacker nevertheless. As she struggled and twisted against the person holding her arms, she felt hot breath against her ear and heard a rough whisper. "That will teach you to send a bird to attack me, witch!"

It was Dennis. Then she heard another familiar voice say, "stop fighting and struggling or I will slit your precious

Isadora's throat." She stopped immediately and looked over. Ralph and Tom had Isadora tied up and Endor was standing over her with a knife. The blade was piercing the skin at her neck causing a thin trail of blood to run down onto the collar of her dress. Kaia froze. She looked to the left and saw Henry holding Isadora's magic amulet up like a knight who was holding up a slain dragon's heart. He had a wicked grin on his face.

He looked at Kaia and sneered, "I knew you were a witch!"
"What do you want?" Kaia asked Endor. "I am nothing to you. I don't belong here nor do you want me here. Let us go and I can promise you will never see me again."
"Let you go?" replied Endor, "Oh no dear Kaia. You see now that Dennis overheard your whole sorry tale earlier; you are now very valuable to me. I wonder how much a King and Queen would pay to see their beloved daughter again – the heir to their kingdom? You are going nowhere. Not until Isadora here helps me contact your family and I have secured a nice sum of gold for your safe return. Until then, the two of you can stay locked upstairs in the attic. Take them away boys."

"She will never help you," Kaia spat as she walked past the woman she had believed to be her mother. "I'll never let her."

"Oh I think you'll find you don't have much choice there, little *princess.*" Endor spat the word "princess" out with so much venom that shivers ran up and down Kaia's spine. "You have caused this family nothing but trouble since your arrival and now you think I'm just going to let you skip off to your castle full of jewels and fancy clothes so you can live happily ever after while we continue to live in poverty. Oh no, your family is going to pay us handsomely for having had to put up with you for the last twelve years. I think that's fair, don't you?"

Kaia didn't reply but felt her blood run cold as she heard how Endor cackled the whole way through the house as they led her and Isadora up to the attic room.

"Henry go and get the chains and shackles." Endor ordered.

"Yes Ma'am," he replied and scurried off as fast as a rat.

"Fitting!" Kaia thought as she looked at Isadora with worried eyes.

A few minutes later they heard the clanking and rattling of chains as Henry dragged them up the stairs to the attic. Endor grinned as she shackled Kaia and Isadora around the wrists and ankles and then attached the long chain to the thick metal handle on the attic trap door. "That should keep the pair of you out of trouble for a while," she said as she ushered everyone out of the rom and down the stairs.

"You'll never get away with this," Kaia shouted after her.

"Oh I most certainly will," Endor replied as she slammed the trap door shut behind her.

Kaia looked at Isadora and got a shock because it looked like she was going to sleep.

"Isadora! What's going on? What are we going to do? You have to zap us out of here quickly," Kaia pleaded.

"It's over Kaia," Isadora said in a tired voice. Her eyes were fluttering shut and she looked like she was struggling to breath.

"What do you mean?" she said, "You're a sorceress. If anyone can get us out of this mess, it's you!"

"Not without my amulet," Isadora said as she took a shuddering breath. "The amulet is my source of power and strength. Without it, I'm just a weak old lady. Now shush Kaia, I need to sleep. I'm so very tired."

"No Isadora," Kaia shouted as she nudged Isadora with her forehead. Her hands were shackled behind her back so she couldn't reach out to her. "Come on Isadora, stay with me. I don't know what to do. I can't do this without you."

As Kaia watched Isadora drift off to sleep, she sighed and slumped down in frustration and then finally hot wet tears streamed down her face as the day's events took their toll on her and she began to cry.

About the author:

An Irish writer of children's fiction and adults academic books, born in 1969 in the Coombe Hospital Dublin, the 5th of 6 children to Joe and Angela Clyne… A Law lecturer and Forensic Psychologist by profession Teresa is as comfortable writing about magic,  dragons and sorcerers as the Irish legal system. Teresa is also a photojournalist having written for many local and national papers and magazines including the Mullingar Advertiser, Irish News Review and Emerald Road Racing.

Teresa Clyne is a **fervent** fan of writing, children's fiction, **dragons and magic**. She loves to create worlds where children and dragons stand side by side in their desire to help make the world a better place. Her heroines often yield magic wands, but Teresa equally values their intelligence, wisdom and compassion. She loves all of the characters in her book but Isadora stands out to her as a selfless and beautiful person, so giving and generous

Please visit Teresa at www.cypathia.com to learn more about her background and interests. Feedback is always appreciated!

READER BONUS..!!

ABSOLUTELY FREE..!!

Cypathia

Part Two: Reunited

by

Teresa Clyne

Chapter 1

The piercing blue eyes staring back at him in the mirror were filled with hope, excitement and if he was honest, just a tiny dash of fear. Today was a very big day. It was his thirteenth birthday and today was the day he met his family for the very first time. Kolby straightened his velvet tunic and watched as Catherine walked across the room with his travelling cloak, made from the finest wool. She helped him to put it on and smoothed down the material over his shoulders.

"You look very handsome," she told him.

"Thank you," he replied as he turned around to look at the woman who had raised him. "Shall we go now?"

"Yes, the portal will be opening soon and then we shall leave at once."

Kolby looked around at the stone cottage he had lived in all his life and felt a little bit sad. He had been happy here.

Although he had been in hiding, he had wanted for nothing. There had been a team of servants who had all been employed by his father and bound by strict magical spells that they could never speak of what they did or what they knew. The cottage itself was protected by a host of enchantments that made it invisible and completely impenetrable by any outside force. There was a lovely garden out back that was also under the same protections where Kolby had become skilled at fencing and heavy armour fighting. He had been taught by his mentor and friend Sir Ghatsby – one of the King's most loyal and talented knights who had agreed to give up twelve years of his life to ensure the prince was properly trained to take on his new role. Kolby had begun learning how to hold a sword at the tender age of three, but it had soon become apparent that he had a natural flair for combat and he had quickly mastered the basics. He had spent many happy days out in the sunshine learning the tricks of the trade and he found nothing more relaxing than to spar with Sir Ghatsby when he needed to let off some steam.

Kolby was snapped out of his daydream when the wall opposite him began to shimmer and wobble and began turning a brilliant silver colour. "Wow," he breathed as he watched the portal form and spread from the middle of the wall right up to the roof and down to the floor. He had known it was going to happen, for Catherine had explained everything to him in great detail, but he was still a bit stunned at the beauty of it as it happened.

"Are you ready?" Catherine asked taking him by the hand and leading him to stand next to her in front of the portal.
"Yes Ma'am," Kolby replied.
"Now remember, whatever happens, DO NOT let go of my hand." Catherine instructed.
Kolby rolled his eyes, "I know!" he told her. "You have told me only like a thousand times since yesterday!"

Catherine smiled at his exasperation. In so many ways he was just a normal teenage boy. "I don't want any more mistakes," she replied. Kolby gave her hand a squeeze. He knew she was haunted by what had happened to his sister and Isadora all those years ago. He heard Catherine shout out in her sleep and knew she had nightmares about it regularly. Catherine had also explained that there was a fifty

fifty chance that he would be going back to ascend the throne as she had no way of knowing what had happened to Isadora and Kaia and even if they had survived she didn't know if they were going to be able to find their way back. As a result, over the last twelve years, Kolby had been groomed not only to be his sister's second in command, but to be the King as well.

He had often heard Catherine complain to the other staff at the cottage that she wished she hadn't done her job quite so well in sealing up the portal. She had tried many times over the years to get a message through to Cypathia to find out what had happened but she had never been able to break through the locking spell. The only way she could have done it was to remove the enchantments from the cottage completely and open up another portal from Kaleseth to Cypathia and that was entirely too risky. She herself was the only person ever allowed to leave the property and that was only once every fortnight when she went to the local village, heavily disguised, to restock their food supply. Catherine was nothing if not thorough and she trusted no-one with Kolby's safety except herself.

She gripped his hand as tightly as she could and stepped forward into the portal pulling Kolby in behind her. He had never felt anything so strange. It was like being squeezed and stretched out like a piece of dough then rolled up again as his legs caught up with the rest of his body. Then stre-e-e-e-e-e-etch again. It was very dark in the portal for a long time and Kolby would have been terrified if he hadn't been hanging onto Catherine's hand with both of his.

Suddenly Kolby felt Catherine stiffen beside him as his ears registered a noise. As the darkness of the portal grew lighter and lighter the noise got louder and louder. Kolby heard shouting and then he heard Catherine tell him to stay behind her as they exited the portal. Kolby noticed the shapes which seemed to be inside the portal but had to time to even consider what they were as in that instant they popped out the other end into dazzling bright light and it took Kolby a few seconds for his eyes to adjust. The shouts were very loud now and they didn't sound friendly or welcoming at all. He looked up and saw Catherine shooting bright daggers of colour out of her fingers and zapping what looked like an entire army of goblins! Instinct kicked in and Kolby reached to his waist, but his sword wasn't there. Catherine had said it wasn't safe to travel through a portal with weapons as the keepers of the portal only allowed unarmed travellers to enter and pass safety, so they had all been left behind and they were going to send someone to retrieve all their belongings once they were settled back in the castle at Cypathia.

In the few seconds of confusion, Kolby felt cold rough hands close around his wrists. He turned around and saw two goblins had seized him from behind. He tried to wriggle free but for creatures that were only half his height they were surprisingly strong and try as he might he just could not wrench his arms free from their grasp. These flat faced, pointy eared and long nosed creatures whose wide mouths when opened showed a set of fang like razor sharp teeth, for even though Kolby was almost twice their size he was no match for their vicious temper and loyalty to King Mordor.

He tried to call out for Catherine but as he opened his mouth he felt his voice die in his throat. Someone had put a spell on him to stop him calling out for help. He looked over to the far wall and saw two humans standing watching the drama unfold. "Sorcerers," he thought, and then he watched helplessly as Catherine battled the goblins alone and he got dragged off down the opposite corridor.

***

Catherine had stunned most of the goblins and was frantically looking around for Kolby when she saw him being dragged off towards the deepest dungeons in the castle. She looked up and met the eyes of a tall broad shouldered man with a long black beard and a bald head. He was wearing a long black robe with red symbols all over it. Catherine didn't have to be able to read the symbols to know they were demonic in nature. He had a short fat man with short red hair standing next to him in the same robes and both were wielding glowing red sticks which she knew were the wands that dark sorcerers used.

Catherine knew she would never get near Kolby with two sorcerers and half an army of goblins in her way and no back up. She had to think and fast. She kept up a steady stream of spells to keep the goblins back and buy her some time. That's when she saw a tiny figure making its way towards her from down the same passage they had taken Kolby.

"Alfrida, no!" Catherine screamed, but the little goblin kept on coming. She ran and dived behind Catherine where she took cover and hastily told Catherine to go back through the portal to safety and to lock it again. Catherine didn't have time to think about what she was doing. She knew she would be no help to anyone if she was captured. She had to escape.

Quick as a flash, she turned around, grabbed Alfrida by the collar of her scruffy pink dress and dived headfirst with the goblin back through the portal. As soon as she was inside she turned to face the circle of light that was the entrance and she zapped it closed and locked it once more.

"Now what?" she thought. "I can't go back to Kaleseth, that's the first place they will look."

119

That's when she heard Alfrida's tiny voice whisper, "Go back to your house in the woods Madam Catherine – at least for now. They don't know where that is."

"Good idea, thanks Alfrida," Catherine told her goblin friend and began performing the spell to create a passage that would take her home diverting it off from the original portal. As they popped out onto her cold stone floor Catherine breathed a deep sigh of relief and nearly choked on the inches of dust covering her old house. It had been thirteen years since she had last seen her home.

"Not to worry Madam Catherine," Alfrida said, "I'll soon get your house spic and span again.

"Never mind that now Alfrida," Catherine replied, "We can't stay here too long anyway. Sit down and tell me everything that's happened."

But before Alfrida could begin her story, there was a loud pop as the portal entrance to her house delivered something in front of the fireplace. Both Alfrida and Catherine just stared in wide eyed disbelief at the unexpected guest.

***

Kaia whistled loudly again and then slumped down on the floor exhausted. She had a special tune that she whistled when she wanted Billow to come and she had been trying to call him for help for hours now and he still hadn't come. Either he was very far away or they had captured him too. She silently swore that if they had hurt one single feather on Billow, she would exact the most fearful revenge and burn their house to the ground - if she ever got out of these blasted shackles.

"Isadora, what are we going to do?" Kaia asked for the hundredth time. "We can't just sit here doing nothing."

Isadora sighed. She was so tired and she just couldn't think straight. "Keep trying Kaia, he'll hear you eventually."

Kaia whistled again and this time she heard a noise far down in the garden. It had to be Billow trying to fly up to the attic window. It was a desperate flapping noise and then a thud over and over again.

"His wings aren't big enough for him to reach us," Kaia said and stomped her foot in frustration. She decided she would have to take a chance if they had any hope of being rescued.

"BILLOW!" Kaia screamed, "Go for help. We are tied up and can't get free. Please you have to find someone to help us. Go quickly Billow, before they capture you too."

Kaia waited and listened and all was still. She crossed her fingers and made a wish that Billow had heard her and somehow would find a way to save them. He was their only hope.

***

Billow heard Kaia's shouts and immediately left. But what was he going to do? The only person who he knew would help Kaia was stuck up there with her. It wasn't like he could just walk to the nearby town and ask someone! Then without knowing why, Billow felt that he needed to go back to Kaia's waterfall. He was sure he would get some inspiration there. He flapped and ran as fast as his little legs and small wings would take him until he reached the place where Kaia had found him. He paced up and down in front of the waterfall wondering what to do. As he looked at the water falling down he was drawn to the bright light coming from behind the water. He made his way over the rocks and carefully walked the path between the cliff and the water. As he rounded the bend he stopped. What was this silvery wall? Billow had never seen anything like it before but he felt a strong pull that he needed to go through it to help Kaia. One part of Billow knew how crazy it was to walk through something when you didn't know where you were going to end up, but he didn't know what else to do and despite it seeming crazy, it just felt right somehow.

Billow could not have been Kaia's best friend for years without some of her fearlessness rubbing off on him so he closed his eyes and dived head first into the silvery substance and hoped that he ended up somewhere useful. He got pushed pulled and squeezed through the portal until finally he saw a spot of light and focused all his attention on moving towards it.

Finally the light got so bright that Billow had to close his eyes. He was squeezed out the other end and dumped in a puff of dust on a cold stone floor. When he opened his eyes and the dust settled, he saw two very confused sets of eyes watching him. One belonged to a lady who had kind eyes and the other belonged to a small grey wrinkled creature who was wearing a terrible pink dress that was far too big for her. They all stared at each other, caught between confusion and alarm. For a minute nobody did anything, then the kind old lady finally broke the silence and said, "you had better tell me who you are and why you are here."

Chapter 2:

Billow sat bolt upright and looked around, dazed and confused but attempting to appear confident and…
ZAAAAAAAAAAAAP!!
A stream of light shot out of Catherine's finger and hit Billow in the throat as she said the words,

"Speak little one so that you may tell,
All the things that in your mind doth dwell"

Billow coughed and spluttered, then cleared his throat and began to speak. His voice was very soft and squeaky and Catherine giggled. "Don't worry," she said, "You'll grow into your voice soon enough. Now tell us your story, little one."

Billow launched into the whole sorry tale, telling Catherine and Alfrida everything he could. "So you see," he finished breathlessly, "You have to help them. They are chained up and I can't reach them. Isadora's amulet has been taken. It's a real big mess!"

"Oh, don't worry too much, little one," Catherine said kindly. "This mess is easily fixed. The hard part lies ahead after we release Kaia and Isadora."

Billow watched with a confused frown as Catherine paced in front of him.

"But what is the best way to do this I wonder. I need to think quickly, we don't have much time."

Catherine walked around the cottage for a few minutes with her hand to her chin pondering and muttering aloud to herself. Alfrida looked at Billow and shrugged. She was quite used to Catherine's ways and remembered them well.

"That's it!" Catherine finally declared and she spun around holding a handful of glowing amber rocks. Billow's eyes widened in alarm and he started to back away from Catherine.

"No don't be afraid, Billow," she told him soothingly. "This is just coal. You have not been eating the correct diet and so you haven't grown properly. This is just to help you. Eating coal will heat up your fire and form a great defense against anyone in your way. It will also allow you to melt things and destroy things that block your path." Billow came forward tentatively and sniffed the rocks in her hand. They were no longer glowing brightly, but were still smoking slightly. "Go on," she encouraged, "they won't burn you."

Billow stepped forward and put the coal in his mouth and what a shock he got! It was the most fabulous thing he had ever tasted in his whole life! He greedily gobbled it up and felt his whole throat and stomach glow with warmth. He felt more alive than he ever had and he looked at Catherine with eyes pleading for more. Before he could ask, she said, "take care Billow. Too much too soon will hurt your throat and might put out your fire for good. No more than a few lumps a day to start with."

Billow nodded his head but his shoulders sagged with disappointment. "Don't worry," Catherine continued, "I have something else for you."

Snarfblatts and pollyworts, dinglepinks and rings,
Are just some of the riches that are fit for kings,
But this little dragon has no use for such things,
What he really needs is a new pair of wings…

And as she said the spell, Catherine moved her hands around in front of her and conjured up a beautiful pair of silvery wings that started out very small in the palm of her hand and as she moved her hands all around they grew bigger and bigger. When the spell was finished, Catherine pushed her hands forward and sent the wings speeding towards Billow where they settled delicately between his shoulders and attached. Billow twisted his neck around in astonishment and slowly gave his wings a shake. He looked back at Catherine, breathed the word "WOW!" and inadvertently sent a stream of fire in her direction. Catherine jumped out of the way just in the nick of time. "Careful Billow," she warned. "You need to be cautious until you have learnt to control your new abilities. Now let's go test out those wings."

They went outside and Billow nervously looked at Catherine for guidance. "Just take off," she told Billow. "You will find it comes naturally."

Billow flapped his wings and began to soar, higher and higher until he was sure he would reach the clouds, then he looped back down to the ground and landed gracefully in front of Catherine.

"Right, shall we go?" he asked.
"No Billow," Catherine said. "It's all up to you now. I have to stay here and make sure the portal stays open and none of King Mordor's goblins come through looking for me. And I need to form a plan for once you have brought Isadora and Kaia here safely."

Billow looked alarmed. "But, but…" he stammered out in his squeaky little voice.
"Don't worry Billow," Catherine reassured him, "You have everything you need to succeed. Trust your instincts and I guarantee they won't fail you."

"Alright," Billow said, not quite as confident as Catherine seemed to be. "I'll be back as soon as I can."

***

Kaia was exhausted. She had fought to stay awake but she had no more strength left and she sagged against Isadora's already limp body and let sleep overtake her. She had no idea how long she had been sleeping for when she heard the most terrible commotion down below in the garden. There was shouting and the sound of things crashing to the floor. It sounded like they were under attack. Kaia shot up, instantly alert and listened carefully. Had the Evil King finally found her? Was he going to take her prisoner and lock her up with the rest of her family? Was this really it? She shook Isadora roughly. "Please Isadora," she begged. "You have to do something to help us. Come on, you have to wake up now!"

But Isadora lay motionless on the ground. The noise was awful downstairs. It sounded as if someone were trying to blow the house down and she could hear the terrified screams of Endor, Iosaf and her brothers. The next minute she heard the most terrible crash right outside the attic window. But that couldn't be right. Who could get up outside the window two floors up?

She heard the tinkle of shattered glass falling on the floor and a loud thump as something landed on the floor near her feet. She realized it was Isadora's amulet lying on the ground in front of her and looked up in surprise to see Billow fluttering like a bird right outside the window. A small hole was visible in the middle of the grime stained window where Billow had tossed through the amulet.

"Oh Billow!" she cried, "My hands are tied. I can't reach it!"

"Lie down Kaia," Billow instructed. "I'll get you out."

Kaia nearly fainted with shock. "Billow!" she shouted. "You can speak!"

"Yeah! Pretty cool huh? Now get down."

Kaia lay down on top of Isadora and waited. The next minute she heard a loud roar and an almighty crash as the glass window shattered. A huge ball of flame shot through the window and flew over her head. She felt the searing heat and couldn't believe that it had come out of Billow.

Billow burst through the hole in the window and ran over to where Kaia lay. He used his sharp claws to cut through the shackles that bound her and did the same for Isadora. "Quick. We don't have much time. Your family are furious. I bought us some time, but I'm sure they will be coming up here shortly. We have to get out of here and to the portal."

Kaia picked up Isadora's amulet and put it over her head so it rested back on her chest and watched as almost instantly Isadora was revived. She sat up and looked at Billow and Kaia. "I'm so sorry," she said. "I have pretended to be merely human for so long now and am not used to having to practice magic. I didn't realize how much I depended on my amulet for strength. I have not been without it before." "It's ok," Kaia said, "I'm just glad to have you back, but we don't have much time. Can you find a way to get us out of here?"

As she spoke she heard the thundering of footsteps coming up the stairs and the sound of angry voices accompanying them. Isadora looked around the room for inspiration and her eyes came to rest on Kaia's old weather beaten rug that covered the middle of the room. She held her amulet in her right hand and pointed it towards the carpet and shouted, "animatus!"

Instantly the carpet began to quiver on the floor and big clouds of dust puffed up into the air. Isadora held her arms out straight in front of her, wiggled her fingers and without breaking eye contact with the carpet began to chant "*Levitus Vestis*" over and over again. Kaia and Billow watched in awe as the carpet slowly lifted off the ground and hovered in the air.

Isadora looked at Kaia with a grin and said, "Well, what are you waiting for? Hop on."

Kaia grinned and climbed up onto the floating carpet. "This is super cool!" she said.

As she settled down and folded her legs, the handle on the attic trap door rattled and the door started to lift up. "Quick Isadora!" shrieked Kaia. She was not prepared to risk being captured a second time.

"Leave it to me," Billow ordered.

As soon as the first pair of eyes peeped up under the trapdoor, Billow let out a stream of fire. Endor screamed and the trap door slammed shut again. "It's that blasted dragon again!" they heard Endor shout down to the others.

Kaia couldn't help herself. She began to giggle. By the time she had helped Isadora up onto the carpet her whole body was shaking the way she was laughing. Isadora settled herself onto the carpet and grabbed the tassels on the front to help her steer. She clicked her fingers and the carpet took off towards the window.

"Have you ever flown one of these before?" Kaia asked.

"There's a first time for everything my dear," Isadora replied with a wink.

"Come on Billow," Kaia said, "Let's get out of here once and for all."

Kaia ducked down as the carpet sailed through the open window and watched as Billow came through after them. The last she saw of Endor was her hanging out the window, purple with rage and shaking her fist after them as they flew off across the rolling green hills and out of sight.

They made it to the waterfall in minutes flying on the carpet. Once they were out of sight of the house, Billow had taken the lead and shown Isadora where to go to find the waterfall and the portal. The carpet landing was a little bumpy and Kaia jumped up rubbing her bottom. "Ouch!" she said with a grin. Despite the sore behind, she had never been happier in her whole life. She was rid of Endor, Iosaf and the horrid people she had called brothers and sisters forever and she was finally off to meet her real family who she knew loved her with all their heart. She could not wait another minute.

"Right," said Isadora, "Show me where this portal is." As soon as she had entered the airspace of Kaia's special place she had felt the magic. She mentally berated herself for never having come to see the place with Kaia over the years, because she felt sure she would have known this was where the portal would materialize and she would have saved herself an awful lot of stress!

Kaia helped Isadora to climb over the rocks and Billow followed behind them until they were standing facing the portal. Isadora grabbed hold of Kaia's hand and instructed her firmly. "Don't let go!"
"I won't," Kaia promised, then turned to Billow and said, "Be sure to stay close Billow."

Billow nodded and they all stepped forward into the portal. Kaia recognised the "Shiny Ones" instantly, their ling thin frames were standing tall and protective as Kaia and Isadora whizzed by, Kaia tugged on Isadora's hand excitedly, Catherine looked around and nodded back with a smile and turned back to ensure safe passage for them both. Kaia waved to the "Shiny Ones" with her other hand and they telepathically said "thank you child, now have a safe journey" back to her.

***

Isadora and Kaia tumbled out of the portal and fell on a hard, dusty stone floor. They heard the thud of Billow landing not far from them. Isadora was the first to stand up and look around in confusion. Before she could say anything, Catherine stepped forward and enveloped Isadora in a big hug. "Isadora," she cried. "It is so wonderful to see you again."

"But, what?" Isadora stammered, "Where are we? Why aren't we at the castle?"

"Come and sit Isadora," Catherine said. "There is much to tell you."

Then Catherine looked past Isadora and her eyes fell onto Kaia for the first time. "Princess Kaia," she whispered. "How lovely to meet you finally."

She gave Kaia a hug too and the three of them went to sit at her kitchen table where Alfrida was already sitting watching them. Billow came and settled himself on the floor next to Kaia and they all looked expectantly at Catherine for some explanation of their surroundings.

"A lot has happened in the last thirteen years," Catherine began, "Alfrida has been filling me in while we waited for you. I think you should start again and tell the princess everything."

Alfrida took a nervous gulp. She was fidgeting with the hem of her dress and looked green under her grey skin. "Well, um…" she began and looked like she was about to burst into tears from nerves.

Kaia reached across the table and took hold of the little goblins hand. "Don't be afraid," she said. "I will make sure nothing happens to you. I need to know what happened to my family."

Alfrida put the back of her hand on her forehead, exasperated and looked up at Kaia with wide saucer-like eyes. "Oh princess, it's all just too terrible for words."

"Just start at the beginning," Kaia said, "and tell me everything."

Alfrida launched into her story and didn't stop to even take a breath until she had finished.

"After you left through the portal the fighting got really bad. King Alexander had called for reinforcements but we were losing soldiers far too quickly and the raven scouts had been out to look – King Mordor's reinforcements were closer than ours. All the goblin servants had taken refuge in the kitchens but we could hear the sounds of war. One of the knights came to tell us that it was every man for himself and we had to run as far and fast as we could to avoid being captured by King Mordor's men. I tried to get away but I wasn't fast enough and I was caught not far from the kitchen. We were all locked up in one cell in the dungeon and still we heard the battle raging on. After what seemed like forever we heard the victory cries of King Mordor's army and we knew King Alexander's castle had fallen. The ravens came to the small dungeon window to tell us that the King and Queen had been taken prisoner. They had been locked up and were under constant guard. Nobody knew what had happened to you and Kolby and a search was underway to find the babies because nobody knew about the portal and thought the minders had just fled with them. The castle was taken over by King Mordor and we were all put to work. As the only female goblin who had been captured, I was tasked as a personal servant to King Mordor and I decided then that I would try to gather as much information as I could. I knew Catherine would be coming back sometime and when she did I wanted to be able to help to free the rightful King and Queen. I pretended to be loyal to the new King and kept my head down and my ears open. King Mordor really didn't bother to be careful when he spoke to his advisors around me and I learned a great deal. They discovered the portal not long after the war ended and he knew someone had escaped with the babies but nobody knew who had them or where they had gone. King Mordor hired a few sorcerers to try re-opening the portal and following you, but nobody could get through Miss Catherine's spell.

That's when he turned to dark magic. He sent his knights out to find Dragmor and Phineas – he had heard rumours that they were the best dark sorcerers in the kingdom and he promised to pay handsomely for their services. The knights tracked Dragmor and Phineas to a demon realm not far from Cypathia called Drungstar, but he could not find a sorcerer willing to open a portal to go fetch them because they were all scared of letting the demons out. He did terrible unspeakable things to the sorcerers who refused him and most of them have gone mad from the torture, but none would do it. He eventually found an old witch who lived deep in a far off forest and managed to tempt her with promises of power once she had opened the portal. She did as he asked and as soon as Dragmor and Phineas were located, brought back to the castle and the portal was closed, he had her beheaded. He set the dark sorcerers to work, but even they could not break Miss Catherine's enchantments, so he did the only other thing he could think of and that was to post a permanent guard outside the original portal opening in the hopes that whoever had taken the babies would try to return.

He knew that the twins would have to return at some point to try to claim the throne and he didn't know if whoever had taken them knew the results of the war. He offered Dragmor and Phineas jobs and with them at his side he became a cruel dictator who is hated by the people.

Over the years, King Mordor's spies have been sent out to try and find out what happened to the twins and it was only about three years ago that one spy reported that only Kolby had made it through the portal and was being guarded in a secret location by someone very powerful. He just assumed Kaia had either been killed in the war or lost inside the portal. He focused all his efforts on finding Kolby but every piece of information he was given led to a dead end. He got more and more frustrated and his anger at being thwarted has led to him becoming a mad and evil man obsessed with power. He so wanted to be more loved than King Alexander and when that didn't happen he became angry and irrational.

King Mordor decided that he would capture Kolby when he tried to return to power and use the dark sorcerers to put a spell on Kolby making him his puppet. This was how he planned to win over the people and he has been obsessed with finding Kolby now for years. It has been hard waiting for your return. When I saw Miss Catherine burst through that portal today, I was so happy because I know that finally we have a chance to free the King and Queen and end King Mordor's reign."

Isadora sat with her hand clamped over her mouth in horror. She couldn't believe the King and Queen had spent thirteen years locked up in a cold dungeon. Kaia just stared down at the floor lost in thought and clearly overwhelmed by the events of the day. She lifted her head finally and spoke. "But where is my brother? He should be here." She looked around as if she was expecting him to suddenly appear through the walls of the cottage.

"He was with me," Catherine said, "But when we came through the portal we were ambushed by King Mordor's goblin guard. While I was fighting them off, he was captured and taken prisoner too."

Kaia sighed loudly. This was an awful lot to deal with. She had been expecting a happy joyful reunion with a family who loved her. She had not been expecting all this drama and now the only thing to do was to go on a rescue mission in order to get her family back.

"How are we going to get to them if there is a goblin army guarding the portal entrance?" Kaia asked. "And even if we get past them, we have no idea where in the castle they are being held. If we go blasting in through the portal, King Mordor is just going to send more guards to fight us off and we will all probably end up captured too."

Alfrida spoke up, "Well luckily you have the best sorceress in Cypathia on your side then. Her magic is unbeatable."
"Thanks for the vote of confidence Alfrida," Catherine commented with a wry smile. "But we are going to need to be clever if we are going to outsmart King Mordor."
"I have faith in you Miss Catherine. If anyone can beat him, it's you."

Isadora looked hopefully at Catherine. "I have so missed you and she is right, you are the best. Do you have a plan?"

"Well as a matter of fact…" Catherine said with a smile. "I actually do."
They all let out a sigh of relief. "I was so panicked about losing Kolby coming back through the portal after what happened all those years ago with Isadora and Kaia that I took every preventative measure I could think of to relocate Kolby if we were separated in the portal."

She pulled a round silver object out of her pocket with a clasp on the one side. She flicked the catch up and pulled out a lock of pitch black hair and held it up triumphantly for all to see.

"Well, that's great," Kaia said impatiently. "I assume that's a lock of Kolby's hair, but we really need the rest of him too!"

She instantly clapped her hand over her mouth, realizing she had said that out loud instead of in her head. The strain of the last twenty four hours was getting to her. Things just weren't going according to plan and she had experienced so much disappointment already in her short life.

"I'm so sorry…" she began, but Catherine held up a hand to silence her and smiled at her kindly.

"Don't worry Kaia," Catherine said, "This little lock of hair is going to lead us to the rest of him after I perform a simple little tracking spell. It will give us his exact location and then we can form a plan to go get him."

She looked around the house as if trying to remember where something was, then went over to the cupboard and pulled out a black ball.

"Oh dear," said Alfrida in alarm. "I'll get that cleaned for you Miss Catherine."

Alfrida quickly set about wiping the ball with a cloth and Kaia saw that it was actually a glass orb. When it was clean, Catherine took it from her and placed it into a metal claw that was in the middle of the table to stop it rolling away while she performed her spell.

"When I cast the spell, Kolby will appear to us in my crystal ball and we will be able to see exactly where he is being held," she told them.

Catherine placed the lock of hair in the palm of her hand and held her hand out in front of her. She began the spell that would lead them to Kolby.

"Lock of hair so black and rare,
Is he here? Is he there?
Help us find the evil lair,

That hides the prince so brave and fair.

Grant him the courage of heart to bear,

Everything until him and Kaia can once more become a pair.

Now reveal his location – show us where!"

The crystal ball began to glow a deep orange colour and slowly inside it they all watched as mist began to swirl, slowly at first and then faster, until it was spinning like a tornado. Then the mist began to dissipate and an image began to form in the orb. It was Kolby and he was sitting on the hard stone floor of what looked like a dungeon. He was sitting hugging his knees to his body and rocking slightly back and forth. As they watched he ran his hand through his hair and looked upwards as if looking straight at them. Kaia felt her heart catch in her chest – THIS was her brother! She felt such a surge of love for him – something she had never experienced for any member of her "other" family before. In that moment she knew she would do whatever it took to rescue him.

Catherine gently removed the orb from the claw and began to turn the crystal ball slowly to get a better view of where he was being held. She moved the orb this way and that looking for any tiny clue as to which dungeon he was in. Then she saw it. A tiny dragon carved into the stone on the floor in the corner.

"That's it!" she declared happily, "I know where he is!"

Chapter 3

"He is being held in the dragon dungeons, deep below the castle. They are used to house captured dragons. They are incredibly well protected," Catherine told them.

"So what are we going to do?" Kaia asked with a worried frown. "It sounds like it will be very difficult to get in there."

"Luckily," said Catherine with a wink. "You have the best sorceress in Cypathia on your side."

They sat for a while trading ideas about the best way to get into the castle unnoticed by the guards. The original portal was obviously out of the question, so they debated whether it was worth opening another portal. Billow offered to blast down the walls with his super-hot fire and Isadora and Catherine considered various spells and enchantments. They only had one chance and they had to get it right.

After some time, Alfrida stood up on the chair and in her tiny voice declared, "I will do it."

"What?" asked Catherine without looking up. She was so engrossed in her spell book that she wasn't really paying attention.

"I'll go and rescue Kolby," she replied.

That got their attention. They all stopped what they were doing and looked up at the tiny goblin with confused expressions.

"How?" Kaia enquired. "You are so little."

"Well if you really think about it, I'm the only one who can enter the castle and be seen without raising anyone's suspicion. I'm *supposed* to be there."

Catherine started nodding her head. "Brilliant!" she exclaimed. "They will never expect that."

"Yeah, she can go inside the castle," argued Kaia, "But once inside how is she going to break Kolby out of a dungeon that is strongly reinforced to hold in dragons?"

"Well she will need a little bit of help," replied Catherine. Slowly, she started to smile. A plan was forming in her mind and she was positive they could pull it off. "Right let's get to work!" she commanded. She flipped through her spell book until she reached the page she was looking for and set the book flat in front of her. She then went and rummaged in the kitchen drawer, pulling out a rusty old metal key. Next she went to her bedroom and returned with a handful of beads and a piece of string. They all watched in confusion as Catherine began threading the beads onto the string and then tied the ends together to make a necklace. Nobody dared to interrupt her while she was working.

She laid the beads out on the table in front of her, pointed her index finger at them and said in a strong clear voice, *"invisibilia"*. A silver light shot out of her fingers and hit the beads causing them to jump off the table and hover in the air for a moment. Everyone jumped as the beads clattered back down onto the wooden table.

Without a word, Catherine picked the beads up and hung them around Alfrida's neck. Almost immediately Alfrida disappeared! Kaia, Isadora and Billow gasped with surprise.

151

"Remove the beads now Alfrida," Catherine said. As soon as Alfrida took them off she reappeared.

"That's how you are going to smuggle Kolby out of the castle," she told the little goblin. "But take care; they will only make him unseen. If someone touches him they will still be able to feel him so you will need to move as quickly and carefully as you can."

Alfrida nodded her head gravely. Nobody had to explain what was at stake here. "But how will I get to him?" she asked.

"With this," Catherine said holding up the rusty key. "I'm going to put an enchantment on it now that will allow it to open up any lock. All you have to do is get down to the dungeons unseen. The key will do the rest for you."

"Ok," Alfrida said. She was feeling brave and terrified all at the same time. If she were caught, she was done for. King Mordor would have her killed for treason. He didn't particularly like goblins to start with. They served their purpose as workers, but that was it.

"We will go with you to the castle as far as the forest and wait for you there. Then we can all go into hiding," Catherine continued.

"I'm ready," Alfrida said and watched as Catherine zapped the key. It changed from being rusty to a bright gold when she was done. Catherine handed her the key and the necklace and she placed them into her pockets.

"Right," Kaia said impatiently. "Shall we get going then?" She was unhappy to be sitting out of the action as she had really wanted to be the one to rescue her brother but deep down she knew this was the best chance of success.

Before they set off on their journey, Catherine put an enchantment on the whole group to disguise them – after all two sorcerers, a human, a dragon and a goblin all marching down the road towards the castle was bound to attract some attention.

They got to the edge of the woods and Catherine looked at Alfrida and told her. "This is as far as we go. We will wait here for you to return with Kolby. Go well my friend and be careful."

They all wished Alfrida luck and settled down behind the bushes to wait. Kaia watched Alfrida's little body get smaller and smaller as she walked off into the distance and wondered if this would be the last time she saw the goblin who was risking her life to save her brother.

***

Alfrida got to the door of the castle kitchen and took a deep breath. This was it and she couldn't mess it up. She walked inside and greeted the chef who was busy preparing a meal. He barely glanced up but when he saw it was Alfrida, he stopped chopping vegetables and said in an irritable voice, "the King has been looking for you. You had better go and see him straight away."

Alfrida's heart jumped into her throat and she scurried off to the King's quarters. Had he seen her? Did he know what she was up to? Was this it – beheading day? When she reached his room, she knocked three times on the door and waited.

"Come in," came the gruff voice of King Mordor.

Alfrida pushed open the door and made her way into the room, careful not to make eye contact and anger him. When she reached him she curtseyed and kept her head bowed as she spoke.

"Yes Master," she said in her tiny voice.

"Where have you been Alfrida? I have been looking for you. I have a special job I wish you to take care of for me as you are my most loyal and trustworthy servant."

"I apologize Master. I have been up in the bell tower cleaning the cannons. I know how you like them to shine and sparkle, "Alfrida said, thinking on her feet.

King Mordor smiled. "You think of everything, don't you?"

"I try Master," Alfrida stammered. Her heart was hammering in her chest and her knees were so wobbly she thought she might fall down at any moment.

"As I said, I have an important job for you," King Mordor continued. "I am not sure if you are aware, but earlier today we finally captured the prince. He is currently being held in the dragon dungeons and I want only you to tend to his needs every day. You are not to tell a soul in this castle where he is being held as I have reason to believe that some are still loyal to Alexander. You will take him food three times a day and a basin of hot water twice a day so that he may clean himself. I do not trust anyone else to do this. You are not to talk to him or answer any of his questions. Do you understand?"

"Yes Master," Alfrida replied. Could it really be this easy? she thought to herself.
"If I find out you have told anyone about his whereabouts within these walls, I will cut out your tongue," King Mordor said with another grin.
"I understand Master," she said aloud.

"Chef is busy preparing his lunch now. You are to go down to the kitchens, collect the tray and then take the back stairwell down to the dragon dungeons. That way you will not be seen or followed. I need his presence kept secret until Dragmor and Phineas have primed him properly," King Mordor told her.

"I will take care of it Master," she told the King and turned around to leave the room.

She made her way down to the kitchens and collected the food tray from the chef. She made her way past the stove and opened the dusty old door that led down the back stairs of the castle. It had become disused during King Alexander's reign as the chef had grown tired of people walking through his kitchen all the time and disturbing his food preparation. After much complaining from the chef, King Alexander had made another stairwell down to the dungeons so the chef could create his culinary masterpieces in peace.

Alfrida hurried down the long corridor and down another flight of stairs until she reached the cold and dark dragon dungeons. Kolby was in the third one along the row – she recognized the hunched over figure. She pushed open the flap and bent down to look through and got an angry voice shouting back at her, "I won't help you people. You can do whatever you like to me but I won't betray my family or the people of Cypathia."

"Kolby," Alfrida began, "You have to listen to me because we don't have much time. I have been sent by Catherine to rescue you. I don't have time now to tell you all the details so you have to just trust me."

There was silence for a minute or two and then she heard a small voice say, "alright, what do I have to do?"

Alfrida used the key Catherine had given her to unlock the huge heavy wooden door. Kolby had to help her to get it open as she was so small and just not strong enough to move such a big object. When they finally got the door open, Kolby just stared at her in amazement. She couldn't have been taller than his knee. "You are going to rescue me?" he asked in confusion.

"Yes!" Alfrida replied a little indignantly.

She quickly told him about the necklace - holding it up in her hand for him to see and told him how it worked. They would have no problems until they reached the kitchen when he would need to be very quiet as they moved past the chef. She had already decided to simply tell the chef that she had to leave the castle so soon after returning as the King had her attending to official business. Kolby nodded his understanding, slipped the enchanted necklace over his head and the two of them set off.

When they reached the kitchen door, Alfrida whispered to the area where she assumed Kolby was standing, "be very quiet now and stay close to me. If we get separated I can't see you to help you. The others are hiding at the entrance to the woods but you need to follow me so I can lead you to the right place."

"Got it," Kolby whispered back.

Alfrida took a deep breath and pushed open the door. She had hoped they would make it back before the goblin clean-up crew had started washing the lunchtime dishes, but the kitchen was full of them, washing, sweeping, mopping and wiping.

"Oh dear," Alfrida thought and sweat started to form on her brow. She hoped Kolby wouldn't bump into anyone. On the other hand the noise might help disguise their footsteps on the stone floor. Alfrida made her way past a counter that was stacked high with dirty dishes and saw the kitchen door that would lead them outside the castle. As she began to pick up her pace, she heard a sound that made her stop in her tracks and turn around.

"Oooof," said a goblin as he walked out from underneath the counter and straight into something that could only have been Kolby's leg. "What on earth was that?" he shouted as he picked himself up off the floor and rubbed his sore head.

He looked around and all the goblins had stopped and were staring at her. "YOU!" one of them shouted. "You're the one who took the Prince's minder back through the portal. What are you doing here?"

"TRAITOR!" another one screamed.

"ALERT THE GUARDS!" yelled a third.

Alfrida froze. Her eyes were wide and she had no idea what to do next. Suddenly she felt something yank her up by scruff of her neck.

"She's floating!" called another. "Get the sorcerers! She is consorting with magicians!"

"Get word to the King at once," the chef ordered and started to walk towards where Alfrida was dangling in mid-air.

With that Kolby opened the kitchen door and began to run. It looked like Alfrida was flying. Nobody knew it was an invisible Kolby making his escape. Faster and faster he ran, making his way to the drawbridge that was open.

Then suddenly Alfrida saw things whizzing past them and looked up. The guard was shooting arrows down at her trying to stop her escaping. "Kolby, you have to hurry!"

"I'm going as fast as I can," he panted.

As he replied, she looked forward and saw the drawbridge being lowered. "We're going to be trapped inside!"

"Quick get onto my back and hang onto my neck," Kolby instructed her and tossed her backwards. She reached out and grabbed for any part of him because she couldn't see him.

"Now hang on," he grunted as he picked up speed. They were moving so fast now that Alfrida just shut her eyes and hoped for the best. If they were caught now, they were done for! Arrows were landing all over the ground and some were getting very close indeed.

Suddenly Alfrida felt Kolby jump and she hung on for dear life. He had grabbed onto the top of the drawbridge as it was being raised. Deftly he flicked his legs over and slid down the other side. He hit the ground with a thud and Alfrida lost her grip on him. "Kolby? Where are you?" she squeaked. "We have to get out of her and fast. It won't be long before King Mordor sends his knights for me."

Kolby took off the beads and picked Alfrida up. "Right show me where to go," he asked her as he began to run again. Alfrida pointed out the right way and then clung onto Kolby's shoulder as she watched the castle get smaller and smaller as they got further away.

***

As they reached the others in the woods, Kaia threw herself at Kolby and gave him the biggest hug she had ever given anyone before. Kolby wrapped his arms around her and hugged her back. After a few moments they broke apart and just stared at each other. Both had so much to say to the other, but neither knew where to even start.

"Okay," said Catherine taking charge, "We are going to have to postpone this reunion just a little longer. If we don't get out of here now, we are all going to have our heads on spokes decorating the castle walls!"

"Everyone join hands and make a circle, quick. Billow you get in the middle. I'm going to have to cast a transportation spell to get us out of here as we will never outrun King Mordor's knights."

Catherine joined hands with Isadora on one side and Kaia on the other, dropped her head and began to chant words that Kaia couldn't quite make out. A wind began to swirl around the outside of the circle, faster and faster. Then, they all began to float with the wind swirling beneath them keeping them up in the air. Higher and higher they soared until they were above the treetops. Kaia heard the knight's horses thundering below them and knew they had gotten out in the nick of time.

"You can all relax now," Catherine said. "We are sitting on a cloud and they cannot see us. As soon as the coast is clear I'm going to use the wind to move the cloud to our secret hide away."

Kaia had never experienced a feeling such as this in her life, the cloud was soft like a feather mattress yet firm, it had a crisp clean smell like the air after a thunderstorm. They waited in silence for what seemed like hours before the noise of the search below them fell quiet. Then Catherine clicked her fingers and the cloud began to move, stealthily transporting them all to safety.

Chapter 4

They soared high over the trees. As they got to the town, Kaia peeped over the edge of the cloud at Cypathia lying below her. They flew over the castle where they saw chaos down below – obviously Kolby's disappearance had been discovered. Then Kaia started to feel very cold. They were approaching a huge mountain range. Catherine snapped her fingers and the cloud rose higher still so that it would clear over the tops of the peaks. She saw Kaia shivering and snapped her fingers again. Kaia looked down in amazement as a beautiful wool coat was now draped over her shoulders. She slipped her arms into it and instantly felt warmer.

"Thank you Catherine," she said sincerely.

"So where are we going?" Kolby asked, unable to contain his curiosity any longer.

"It's not much further," Catherine said. "We are going to a faraway forest that is believed to be haunted."

"Haunted?!" said Kaia and Kolby at the same time.

Catherine laughed. "You two are already thinking the same thoughts," she said affectionately. "Don't worry, the forest is not really haunted. It's just that it is on the outskirts of Cypathia where people don't often go. There were a few people who set off to explore the mountains and the forest beyond many years ago and they never came back. That's how the rumors started. But most likely they died of cold or got eaten by a bear in those treacherous mountains. We will be quite safe where I'm taking you as not many are brave enough to try cross the mountains."

"But what about King Mordor's sorcerers?" Isadora asked. "They will use dark magic to come find us."

"Yes Miss Catherine," Alfrida agreed, "I've seen them at work. They are cruel and scared of nothing. They won't rest until they have found us."

"Well, its lucky then that I have a few friends deep in those woods who have prepared a super-secret bunker for us to hide away in while we perfect our plan to overthrow King Mordor."

"But how?" asked Isadora, "How could you have known? When did you even have time to contact anyone since we have been back?"

"Isadora my dear, do you not know me at all?" Catherine said with a wink.

***

They made it over the mountain peaks and began to descend. They floated over a bright emerald green canopy of treetops. It reminded Kaia of her special waterfall back in Herecia. Catherine leaned over the edge of the cloud and sent a stream of green stars out her fingers. The stars settled on the treetops whose leaves gently opened. Catherine maneuverer the cloud down through the space and landed on the soft moss that coated the floor. She snapped her fingers and the cloud disappeared.

"We will have to continue on foot," Catherine said. "It's not far."

They all set off following Catherine through the overgrown forest. Kaia and Kolby looked at each other in confusion a few times as Catherine knocked on random trees along the way. Finally they came to a rocky pathway. Kolby took hold of Kaia's hand and helped her along so she didn't fall. It felt so lovely to be cared for.

The path veered off into more bush and after what felt like an hour of walking, Catherine finally said, "We're here!"

They all looked around. They didn't appear to be anywhere different to where they had been for the last hour. The floor was covered in moss and there were trees all around them. Billow snorted and a stream of smoky flames shot out his nostrils. Kaia nudged him and whispered, "behave."

Catherine raised her hand straight up so it was pointing to the sky. A silver star shot out of her finger and hovered in the air for a few seconds. "That's a seeking star," Isadora told Kaia and Kolby. "It helps you find things you have lost."

A moment later, the star shot forward and attached itself to the trunk of a huge tree. "Ah, there it is," said Catherine and she motioned for the others to join her. She placed her hand onto a knot on the tree trunk and rubbed it and suddenly a doorway opened. Catherine looked at everyone with a smile. "Well, what are you waiting for? In you go," she ordered making ushering motions with her hands.

They all looked at each other and then obeyed. As they entered, they saw that there was a long winding staircase leading down beneath the ground. "Quickly now," Catherine said impatiently. "I need to seal this back up and cast my protective enchantments to keep any unwanted visitors out. Isadora, please cast an illumination spell so I can close up here."

Isadora snapped her fingers and suddenly light flooded the tree trunk. Kaia looked around to see torches burning brightly with flames lighting the way down the stairs.

"Now just follow the stairs to the bottom. I'll meet you there in a few minutes," Catherine told them.
They walked carefully down the stairs in single file until they came to the end. The stairs opened up onto a huge

room with six pathways leading off from the main room. The room was kitted out with what looked like hand carved wooden furniture and was very simply decorated.

"What is this place?" Kaia wondered out loud.
At that moment Catherine stepped off the bottom of the staircase and grinned. "Isn't this place great?" she asked.

"It really is," answered Kolby. "But where are we?"
"This bunker was used as a safe house during the gnome revolution a century ago, but that's a story for another day," Catherine said absentmindedly running her hand through her hair. "Since then, it has been kept as an underground place of safety for magical folk in trouble. Housekeeping is taken care of by the faeries so that's why it is so clean."

"So how do we know we are safe and won't be discovered?" Kaia asked.
"Because I know some very powerful faeries who have granted us permission to stay here. They too have suffered under King Mordor's reign and want him out. While we

were in the woods waiting for Alfrida, I was able to get a message to my faerie friend, who was able to get things organized for us to stay here for as long as necessary. Now before we start hatching any royal rescue plans, we all need to get some food in our bellies and some rest."

Catherine snapped her fingers and piping hot bowls of stew and fresh bread appeared on the table. Famished after all the adventure, everyone sat down and ate hungrily. Poor Billow just lay down on the mat by the fire place and let out a sigh.

Catherine gave his head an affectionate rub. "You don't think I forgot about you Billow?" she asked. She snapped her fingers and a huge bowl of meat appeared in front of him, the likes of which he had never seen before. Next to the bowl were six glowing coals. "Just a little something for dessert," she told him with a wink.

When dinner was over and everyone had eaten way more than they should have, Catherine ordered them all down one of the passages, as she circled her magic wand around and around, deep purple rays shot from the end of the wand. With each circular motion a cascade of beds magically appeared in the passage, until there was one for everyone. Catherine told them to climb into bed and sleep. Kaia looked longingly at Kolby. She had so much she wanted to talk to him about. They had met a few hours back, but with all that had been going on, she hadn't really had any alone time with him. Sensing Kaia's reluctance to go to bed, Catherine very firmly steered her into a small bedroom with a beautiful purple quilt on the bed. In the corner was a wash stand and there were three torches on the walls.

"Not now child," Catherine told Kaia. "There will be plenty of time to get to know your brother. Now you need to rest."

"But, how did you…" Kaia began, but then stopped herself. She had a feeling Catherine wasn't going to be quite as easy on her as Isadora had been over the years. For the first time in years, Kaia decided to hold her tongue and simply do as she was told. Besides, it was nice to have someone fuss over her and take care of her needs for a change.

Spontaneously Kaia turned, gave Catherine a big hug and then climbed into bed. "Goodnight," she whispered as the door shut behind her.

Chapter 5

The next year went by in a blur. Catherine and Isadora looked at various plans and strategies and the best way to reclaim the Kingdom and free the King and Queen. Kaia and Kolby bonded really quickly and became inseparable. They did everything together and were the best of friends. Kolby took Kaia under his wing to teach her everything he had been taught about royal life. He had been brought up differently because in Kaleseth he had not needed to keep his identity a secret. Kaia really struggled at first with 'being proper'. She had never been allowed to eat at the table, let being shown the niceties like table manners and etiquette. Kolby also set about training her physically. She was so small from being malnourished but was surprisingly strong for her slight build. He worked with her, showing her the skills for heavy armour fighting and archery. He was pleased to see that Kaia was a quick student, picking up the fighting arts with ease.

Kaia also had lessons twice a week with Catherine and Kolby so she could learn the politics of royalty and how to be a good leader. Kaia really struggled with these classes because she had never been exposed to royal life and found the responsibility she was facing as the future ruler of the Kingdom quite overwhelming. On more than one occasion, she told Catherine to just let Kolby do it. She argued and fought for him to be the King, but that was another thing they had to help her to understand. The law was strict. The first born child of the King, a boy or a girl, had to ascend to the throne. She had tried arguing that she was only older by a few minutes and would it *really* make that much difference when Kolby was such a natural?

In turn, Kaia taught Kolby how to rough it. She taught him how to tell if fruits, nuts and berries in the forest were poisonous or edible. She showed him how to climb trees and be barefoot outdoors. At first he was horrified, but he slowly started to loosen up and the two of them had great fun romping in the section of the forest that Catherine had sealed with her magic. Kaia knew that she should enjoy this kind of wandering off while she could as once she was

175

Queen, she would never be allowed to run wild outside and get dirty. This was what bugged Kaia the most about her new role. She had always been so free in Herecia. She didn't have to answer to anyone and she had been pretty much allowed to come and go as she pleased. The weight of the responsibility that was awaiting her weighed down on her and the only person she felt comfortable expressing her fears to was her brother. She knew she had him to lean on and to help her and that gave her a lot of comfort.

After about six months in the forest, Catherine came to Kaia one day with a serious face. "Kaia, I need to speak with you," she said.

Kaia had been alarmed. She had been convinced that it was going to be bad news and she just honestly couldn't handle anything else going wrong.

"Billow is your soul mate," she began earnestly. "I see the bond the two of you have, most especially now that you can talk to him. However, Billow is also integral to our rescue attempt. I have been consulting with the Faerie Queen, the rebel goblins as well as the Gnome General who all feel that without dragons on our side, we don't have a hope of overthrowing King Mordor."

"But Billow is so small still," Kaia protested. "How is he going to help us?"

"He has grown considerably," Catherine said. "But he needs to grow more and he needs to be trained in combat. He needs to learn to fly to attack and he needs to learn effective evasive manoeuvres for when the King's Guard opens fire on him."

At this Kaia had burst into tears. "I don't want him to be in any danger," she had sobbed.

"With the proper training, he won't be in danger. He will be a valuable weapon," Catherine assured her. "I wouldn't be suggesting this if there was another way."

"What do you want to do to him?" Kaia asked between sniffles, "Who is going to train him?" Rubbing her hands along his beautiful white feathers, Kaia felt a rush of love and protection for Billow that she had never felt for any living being before.

"I have managed to send word via magic to the mountain dragon clan. They are believed to be the fiercest and most dangerous dragons in the world. They have been outlawed in the kingdom and generally keep to themselves in the mountains. I sent the message via the universal sign for peace, a dove, a few weeks ago. They have been so badly persecuted and blamed over the years for misdeeds they do not do business with humans at all. I had all but given up hope when Thor, their leader, sent me a message back yesterday."

"You are going to send poor Billow to a clan of killer dragons?!" Kaia had screeched. "Are you crazy?" Her stomach gurgled with anticipation and fear. She bit her bottom lip nervously as she imagined all sorts of ill fates which could befall Billow from these killer dragons.

"Kaia, calm down child," Catherine had soothed as she reached out and touched Kaia's arm. "There is no danger to Billow. He is one of them and they would never harm their own. The people are terrified of them because they are believed to be wild, unpredictable and ferocious but they have been wrongly accused of many things over the years and they have an unjust bad reputation. None of it is true. I would never send Billow into any known danger."

Kaia breathed and then started to cry again. "I could never handle it if something happened to Billow. The heart ache would kill me!"

Catherine stroked her face tenderly and said, "they are going to get him strong for us. They are going to teach him to hunt properly. They are going to show him how to take down big animals like deer and bears. I can only help him so much by feeding him coal and he isn't growing quickly enough. With their help, he will be a full grown dragon by the end of the year. He will learn not only to hunt but he needs to know how to turn his prey black before eating it as the ash and charcoal will strengthen him and allow him to grow faster. There is a fine art to this practice. If he blackens his prey too much he will grow too fast for his skeleton and it will cause his bones to break. If he doesn't blacken it enough, it will stunt his growth forever. I am good at magic, but even I need help from the experts from time to time. Billow will be in good hands with Thor. I promise."

And so with a heavy heart Kaia had agreed to let Billow go. She had watched sadly as he flew off to the arranged meeting place in the mountains. She knew it was for the best, but it still didn't make it any easier. Billow's absence awakened a new kind of fierceness in Kaia. She attacked her studies with renewed vigour and became a formidable fighting opponent. She had even managed to beat Kolby once or twice. When she had teased him good naturedly about losing to a girl, Kolby had joked back that he had let her win. This had led to a friendly competition between the siblings which had seen them both grow in speed, strength and accuracy.

Kaia also spent time every day with Catherine and Isadora honing her magical ability and learning to control her powers. She had been delighted to learn she could do magic and was so excited when she got spells right. Catherine was trying to teach her simple defensive magic spells simply for her own protection when the time came to attack the castle. She would have to undo many years of training if they pulled off the attack before she could use her magical ability spontaneously. This was Kaia's favourite part of the day and she concentrated hard to be able to get it right. She liked the idea of being able to protect the ones she loved. She had her magic and Kolby had his swords and together they were becoming an unstoppable team. She knew that when Billow returned, they would be a forceful trio that would stop at nothing until her parents were freed.

***

The day of Kaia and Kolby's birthday dawned sunny and bright. Kaia was so excited. This was to be her very first proper birthday where she could celebrate with people who loved and cared for her. She bounded down to the kitchen and when she saw Kolby sitting at the table she rushed over and gave him a huge hug. He hugged her back affectionately and the two of them sat together eating breakfast. They watched totally amused as Isadora wrestled with a magic spell to make them a cake. She just couldn't seem to get it right. It was either lopsided or flat. One time it was even upside down on the plate hovering in mid-air! Kaia and Kolby sat together giggling, try after try the cakes became more like a troll had taken a bath in them, suddenly the laughter could not be held any longer, both laughed until they cried., until eventually Catherine felt sorry for her and came over to help. She snapped her fingers and the most exquisite cake Kaia had ever seen sat in the middle of the table. It was lime green and lilac with a golden crown perched on top.

"Wow!" Kaia said loudly.

"Amazing!" said Kolby.

"Thank you," Catherine said with a smile. "I'm glad you guys like it."

"The only thing missing today is Billow," Kaia said sadly. "I really wish he could be here to celebrate with me. Do you know when he is coming back?"

"I have not heard from Thor in two weeks," Catherine said and quickly hurried out of the kitchen.

"Mmmmmm," said Kolby.

"What does that mean?" Kaia asked her brother.

"It means I know Catherine and she is up to something!" he replied. "I wonder what it could be."

Kaia didn't want to spend too much time thinking about serious things today. She simply wanted to enjoy her birthday. "Come on Kolby," she said grabbing him by the hand, "Let's go climb the tree and enjoy the sunshine."

The two of them hurried out of the bunker and began to climb up the tree. They swung themselves up through the branches until they were right near the top. They settled on their favourite branches and sat admiring the view.

"Cypathia really is beautiful," Kaia said. "I wonder what it would have been like to grow up here."

Kaia often spoke about 'what could have been'. Kolby allowed her to because he knew what a rough time she had growing up and even though he knew it wasn't his fault, he still felt guilty that he had been the one that had the better upbringing.

He turned to his sister and said what he usually did. "It will all be over soon. We won't fail in the take over and mum and dad will be free and we will have a wonderful life. I promise you, nothing will ever separate us again."

As they sat in the tree Kaia saw something in the mountains. She rubbed her eyes because surely she wasn't seeing what she thought she was. She turned to Kolby.

"Did you see that?"
 "See what?" he replied.
"Over there in the mountains," Kaia said pointing to the snowy peaks. "It looked like a huge ball of flame being shot up into the air."

Kolby watched the mountains where Kaia had indicated and sure enough another great ball of fire erupted into the air. Against the snowy white backdrop of the mountains, she couldn't miss the gigantic ball of orange-red flame.
"I hope that doesn't mean trouble," Kolby said. "We had better go and tell Catherine and Isadora.

They swung themselves down through the branches with agility and ease and came bursting through the door to the bunker only a few minutes later.

Isadora and Alfrida were in the kitchen setting up the table for lunch and looked up in alarm at the noise.

"Where's Catherine?" Kaia burst out. "We need to see her now."

"Calm down Kaia," Kolby said patiently. "We don't know if it means anything just yet."

"Catherine isn't here," Alfrida told them. "She went out a while ago to get supplies."

Kolby and Kaia looked at each other in alarm.

"What's wrong?" Isadora said. "Tell me, maybe I can help."

Kaia and Kolby spilled out the story of what they had seen in the mountains and explained that they were worried there might be trouble.

"Okay," said Isadora calmly, "Let's go outside and see what's going on."

As they climbed the stairs Kaia's heart was beating frantically in her chest. She just hoped Billow was alright. If something happened to him, she would never forgive herself.

Isadora pushed open the door carved into the tree trunk and stepped out into the sunshine. She got the shock of her life.

There was Catherine standing in the clearing waving her arms about and as she did, the canopy of trees parted baring the sky. Kaia looked up and saw a huge white dragon circling in the air above.

"Happy Birthday Kaia," Catherine said.

Kaia looked up again and realised it was a full grown Billow, returning at last. A flurry of happiness flew through her and tears filled her eyes. This was THE best birthday present ever! She was so happy. Billow landed and Kaia rushed over to him and threw her arms around his neck. For the first time ever, Billow was bigger than her. It felt strange and wonderful all at the same time.

"Billow, I'm so glad you're home," Kaia said.

"It's good to be back," Billow replied.

Even his voice had changed. Gone was the quiet squeaky voice and in its place was a deep ringing.

"There is so much to tell you," Billow said, "But first I want to introduce you to someone."

Kaia, Kolby, Isadora, Catherine and Alfrida watched as Billow tilted his head up to the sky and shot a fireball out of his mouth straight up into the air. As soon as the flames and smoke disappeared they all saw another dragon circling overhead. This one was bright purple and seemed to be slightly smaller than Billow was. The purple dragon landed and Billow looked over with so much affection that Kaia felt her breath catch.

"What on earth is going on?" Kaia wondered quietly to herself. She looked over at Catherine and it was clear by her face that she hadn't been expecting this dragon either.

"This is my friend Indi," Billow said. "She has a proposal for you."

"Well, this is most unexpected," Catherine said. "Let me just secure the area with a magic spell so we can't be heard, seen or traced. Clearly you two won't fit down the tree trunk!" she added with a chuckle as she began to wave her arms around sealing them all inside a protective bubble.

"Right, so what's your proposal?" she asked. "It's safe to talk now."

Chapter 6

"I come to you on behalf of the mountain dragon clan on the orders of our clan leader Thor," Indi began.

"Uh oh!" Kaia thought, "This can't be good!"

"Alright," Catherine said warily. She really hoped she hadn't somehow offended Thor. They could not afford to have the mountain dragons as enemies at this stage of their plan.

"Thor would like to offer you a partnership," Indi continued. "He would like to work with you to get rid of King Mordor."

Catherine couldn't hide her shock. He mouth fell open and she just stared at the purple dragon, totally at a loss for words. It was completely unheard of for the mountain dragons to even contact humans, never mind ask to work together with them towards a common goal. The dragons had been so persecuted over the years that they just kept to

189

themselves and avoided humans at all costs. Catherine had taken a huge chance contacting him to ask for Billow to go train with them and she had been really surprised when they had agreed. This was so unbelievable and unexpected that for once she didn't know what to say.

Billow and Indi exchanged a glance. Billow had only spent a little time with Catherine but he had never seen her look so dumbstruck before.

"Madam Catherine," he said, "This is good news. I thought you would be pleased."

"But… but…. How?" Catherine stammered out.

"Well Indi and I got to be really good friends during my time with the mountain clan and she asked lots of questions about my life before. I told her all about the evil humans and about what King Mordor had done to Kaia's parents and the horrid life she had because of it. Through my stories, Indi realized that not all humans were evil and not all humans thought that dragons were bad. She approached Thor and started telling him the things that I was telling her. Somehow she managed to soften him and one day he admitted that he had once enjoyed a good relationship with humans. He used to be part of the King's Guard a century ago but then a war had broken out and a new King had taken over – one who HATED dragons. And that was where all the trouble started. All the dragons were outlawed and banished to the mountains and told never to return or they would face death. The people were turned against dragons and horrible stories were made up and fed to the people under the new King's reign. These stories have just been passed down and that's why people are so scared of us. Indi and I made Thor realize that he could enjoy the same relationship again with humans if we could only free Kaia's parents and allow Kaia to ascend the throne."

"Well of course," Kaia interrupted. "Dragons aren't scary! I would never banish them to the mountains."

"I know Kaia," Billow said kindly. "And now Thor knows too. I told him all about you and how you have taken care of me since I fell out of my nest as a baby."

"I think he always regretted not fighting for his kind all those years ago and just retreating to the mountains for a quiet life," Indi said. "He doesn't want to hide anymore and wants to help us get rid of the evil King Mordor because he reminds him of the awful King who sent him away all those years ago."

"Wow!" Catherine said. "Well this is fantastic news. Of course we will partner with the mountain dragons. Does he have a plan? Is he coming here for a meeting?"

"No," said Indi. "I am under orders that if you agree, I am to take you to him immediately to formulate an attack plan. If you do not agree, I am to return alone and he will have nothing more to do with humans ever again!"

"Well then," said Catherine rubbing her hands together determinedly, "I had better go and get my winter travelling cloak. It's cold up in those mountains at this time of year."

"Don't worry Miss Catherine," said Alfrida quickly, "I'll go and get it for you." And with that she scurried off back down the staircase into the bunker. She returned a few moments later with a red travelling cloak with gold around the borders.

Catherine put the cloak on, turned to Indi.

"Hop on," Indi said bending herself right down onto the floor so Catherine could climb onto her back. Catherine settled herself between Indi's wings on her shoulder blades and held onto her neck feathers.

"Ready?" Indi asked.
"I'm ready," Catherine said.

Indi began to flap her wings and rose slowly up through the gap in the trees. As she began to soar higher and higher, Catherine sent down a stream of silver rain that closed the canopy of trees once more. The last the people on the ground heard was Catherine shouting, "see you all soon!"

***

Catherine returned a week later with a parchment scroll and a big smile on her face. They were all sitting around the table in the kitchen when she came down the stairs and casually joined them.
"Well?" said Isadora.

193

"It's going to be a piece of cake," Catherine said as she unrolled the scroll and showed them the battle plan. "We attack at dawn three nights from now after the full moon."

"Why wait?" said Kaia impatiently. "Let's go in the morning."

Kolby laughed and nudged his sister good naturedly with his elbow. "Still so patient I see," he told her sarcastically.

Kaia stood up, stomped her foot and shouted, "I've waited patiently my whole life! I'm tired of waiting now! It's time to do something. I can't stand just sitting here and doing nothing for another minute!"

"Kaia dear," said Catherine soothingly. "We have to wait until the full moon. The dragons are at their strongest then because their fire is hottest. Our whole plan rests on them. We need all the help we can get."

Kolby pulled on Kaia's hand which was trembling until she sat down and sighed heavily. "I guess you're right," she conceded. "I'm just a bit frustrated."

"It will soon all be over," Catherine told her. "It's not much longer."

***

The night before the attack was due to take place, Catherine made everyone a sleeping draught in the late afternoon. "We have an early start tomorrow and we all need to be well rested and alert," she said. "You all know what you have to do and this plan is going to work. Now drink up and let's all get some sleep."

With hands clasped around the draught cup, Kaia felt a rush of fear. Her bones felt cold from the inside out, like they were brittle and about to break. Leaning forward, Kolby reached out a tentative hand, wrapping his arms around Kaia's shoulders. Kaia looked up at Kolby, her heart pounding, her lips pensively pressed together. Kolby anxiously pictured himself protecting his sister; he was after all a jousting, heavy armour and fencing champion.

Kolby wrapped his arms around Kaia and whispered, "don't be afraid, we are all here together. I will take care of you. Sip your draught and let's sleep for we will need our rest to win our battle". Kaia drifted off to sleep, still dressed.

She woke in the darkness with a start, sitting bolt upright and calling Kolby. Kolby tiptoed across the white marble floor, sat on the side of her bed and gently stroked her head. Kaia felt protected and drifted back to sleep.

***

Catherine woke them all up while it was still dark outside. They had everything they needed already packed and everyone got dressed into their protective battle gear in silence. A wave of relief swept over Kaia. The mood was anxious, tense and hopeful all at once.

They climbed the stairs up the tree trunk and stood in the cool night air waiting. It wasn't long before Catherine performed the spell to bend back the tops of the trees and open the canopy for Billow and Indi.

"We're all set," Billow said. "Are you guys ready?"

Kaia and Kolby both had the same determined set to their jaws and nodded their heads briskly.

"We're ready," Isadora said confidently. She was so glad to finally have a chance to put right what she had done wrong all those years ago and was determined that this plan should work so she could give Kaia the life she deserved and had missed out on for fourteen years.

"Alfrida," said Catherine taking the little goblins hand in hers, "You have been invaluable to this team, but I want you to stay here. It's going to be a ferocious battle and I don't want you hurt. When we are victorious I will come back and fetch you. You will find everything you need inside your room. I have prepared plenty of supplies for you."

"No Miss Catherine!" Alfrida shouted in her tiny voice. "I want to come too!". She banged her little hand on the table in frustration.

"I'm sorry," Catherine said. "It's too dangerous."

As she said the last words, she sent a stream of red light at Alfrida which hit her square on the chest freezing her in place with her mouth wide open in protest.

"What are you doing Catherine?" Isadora exclaimed!

"It's a temporary spell to turn her into a statue," Catherine said calmly. "It's for her own protection. She is so small and will be an easy target for King Mordor's forces to capture. If they have a bargaining tool, it will make this all a little harder. I knew she would never agree to stay behind willingly and I couldn't take a chance that she would try to come with us. It's just easier this way. She will remain a statue for an hour and then she will unfreeze. That will give us enough time to get far enough away so that she cannot follow us."

Catherine went over to Alfrida and kissed her on the head. "I know you can hear me still and I hope I have explained my actions so that you won't be too angry with me. Please try to understand. We will see you again soon."

"Right," she said. "Let's not waste another minute. We have a kingdom to reclaim!" Catherine and Kolby climbed onto Indi's back and Kaia and Isadora climbed onto

Billow. The two dragons took off towards the mountains. The currents of warm air under their large wings raised the dragons up over the clouds. Kaia had never felt so free in her entire life. Looking down, she could see the forests, valleys, fields, rivers and mountains of Cypathia, each snowy mountain top passing like a shimmering blur.

They passed through the occasional cold and foggy cloud, giving Kaia goose bumps. Not scary goose bumps like she had on many occasions as a child at the hands of her family, but excited goose bumps, the good kind. This was where she belonged. At one with Billow with her blood flying next to her. She was exhilarated and excited for the battle that lay ahead. She turned around to look at Isadora who looked terrified.

"Are you scared?" she asked Isadora.
"A little," Isadora admitted. "Are you?"

"I'm not scared," Kaia said. "I'm angry and I'm ready to take back what's mine!"

***

Finally, they arrived in Gaigue Mountains in just a few short minutes on the backs of the massive dragons. When they landed they found no fewer than a dozen dragons waiting for them. Thor was standing off to the one side. He was a ginormous red dragon who looked terribly fierce. He came forward slightly and bowed his head to Kaia.

"Greetings future Queen," he said in a gruff voice. "I hope to have many happy dealings with you."

Kaia bowed her head in return. "Greetings Sir," she said. "I hope so too."

"I trust you have been informed of the plan?" Thor asked.

"Yes I have," Kaia replied. "We are all ready."

"Then let's not waste another moment," he said. "Here are my best warriors. They are ready for battle."

Catherine slid down off of Indi's back and approached the line of dragons. She held up her hands and began to weave them in complicated patterns while muttering an incantation.

"That's a concealment spell," Isadora whispered to Kaia. "We don't want to give them any warning that we are coming."

As Catherine finished her spell, the dragons became transparent and took on the appearance of their surroundings. Only a very faint outline of them was remained. Kaia and she knew that they wouldn't be spotted from the ground. It was to allow them to get close enough to attack by surprise.

Next Catherine came over and performed the same spell on Indi and Billow, before hopping back onto Indi's back behind Kolby.
"Thank you Thor," Catherine said. "I hope we shall all return with good news shortly."

With that, the dragons all took off into the air and began circling in the sky as they got into their battle formation.

Kaia looked over and caught Kolby staring intently at her. He gave her a thumbs up sign and mouthed the words,

"Love you sis," before clutching the hilt of his sword and focusing straight ahead.

The dragons flew steadily on to the woods on the outskirts of the city – the same woods where Kaia had waited for Kolby a year ago. Once they flew over the city boundary, all the dragons let out a large snort and sent clouds of billowing smoke in the direction of the castle to further hide their approach.

Just seconds later, complete and total chaos erupted as 12 warrior dragons began unleashing their assault. They flung humongous fireballs out of their mouths and at the castle walls. They had been instructed by Thor to avoid hurting any humans but to just cause confusion and mayhem so that Isadora, Catherine, Kolby and Kaia could get to the dungeons to rescue the King and Queen.

The twelve warriors perched on the castle walls and rounded up much of the goblin army in just a few minutes using fireballs. Some more dramatic descriptions of the battle would be a good idea – some of the sights, sounds, smells etc. This again is a dramatic moment. They held them in a corner of the castle courtyard, while Billow and Indi flew in with the royals and their sorcerers. The goblins were furious but they knew they were beaten.

Billow and Indi landed safely in the courtyard and Catherine indicated the way to go. As they entered the castle, Catherine turned to the dragons and said, "see if you can find King Mordor, Phineas and Dragmor. They will be around here somewhere."

Catherine, Isadora, Kaia and Kolby headed as quickly as they could down to the dungeons where Alfrida had told them the King and Queen were being held. The few goblins that remained inside the castle scattered and ran when they saw the four headed their way.

"Goblins are notorious cowards!" Catherine muttered to the rest of them. "Only happy to fight if they outnumber you and are likely to win."

"What about the evil sorcerers?" Kaia asked. "Will they come out and fight?"

"I hope not," Kolby said. "My first run in with them did not go very well."

They crept quickly and stealthily through the castle. Catherine, Isadora and Kaia had their wands at the ready and Kolby clutched his favourite fighting sword. As they came around the one corner they heard a commotion inside one of the rooms and raised voices.

Catherine motioned for them all to stop and put her finger to her lips in a gesture of keeping quiet. They listened for a few minutes before Catherine said, "that's King Mordor and he is arguing with the sorcerers, I'm sure of it."

They all looked at one another as they struggled with the dilemma. Did they carry on down to the dungeons and risk allowing King Mordor to escape? Or did they enter into battle with him now and run the risk of being hurt and killed, thereby losing the opportunity to rescue the rightful King and Queen?

Catherine turned to Kaia. "It's your call," she said. "You are going to be Queen when this is all over. What do you want to do? Go in or move on?"

Kaia looked at Kolby and met his eyes in a meaningful look. They had developed the most incredible bond over the months where they seemed to know what the other was thinking without either of them uttering a word.

Kaia straightened her back and squared off her shoulders. "We go in," she told them. "I can't risk letting the vermin who have destroyed my life get away. We fight!"

"Right then," with a short sharp gasp Catherine said. "Here's what we do." At this Isadora, Kaia and Kolby stepped closer.

Chapter 7

The four of them stood in front of the door, wands and sword at the ready. Catherine aimed her wand at the door, ordered "get down," and then muttered an incantation.

The next minute there was an almighty crash as the door exploded off its hinges in a cloud of purple smoke. Catherine led them into the room through the smoke and she, Isadora and Kaia started firing off spells hoping to hit something while the dust settled.

There was lots of shouting and Catherine knew she had caught King Mordor off guard. It was what she had been hoping for so she could disarm the sorcerers before they could do any damage to the four of them. As they came inside, King Mordor made a dash for the door. Catherine and Isadora fired spells but missed. He was ducking and diving behind the furniture trying to make his way to the door. He dived behind a large sofa and narrowly missed being hit by a jet of red light that Kaia fired at him.

"Quick!" shouted Isadora, "Zap the sorcerers!"

As Catherine turned her attention back to Dragmor and Phineas, she saw them turn to face one another and aim their wands. This was what Catherine had feared. She had worried that they would use complicated dark magic to hide themselves or simply to just zap each other back to some far away demon realm where they could never be found.

"Isadora!" Catherine yelled, "Cast a metamorphosis spell."

The two women turned to focus on the two men who were waving their arms around and chanting spells without breaking eye contact.

Catherine and Isadora threw their spells at the sorcerers at exactly the same time that they threw their spells at each other. The four spells collided, sending colourful jets shooting out in every direction. Catherine, Isadora, Kaia and Kolby dropped to the floor, but Dragmor and Phineas were not quick enough and got hit by a few different spells.

As the dust of the battle settled and the foursome got to their feet, they saw that both sorcerers had been partially turned into rats. Dragmor's long beard remained and when he tried to scurry out the door Kaia stomped her foot down on it, stopping the rat in his tracks. She picked him up by the scruff of his beard, zapped him with a freezing spell and slipped him into her pocket. She looked over to see that Phineas too had been changed into a rat, but he was still wearing his long robes so every time he tried to run he tripped on the robes so he couldn't get very far. Isadora zapped him with a freezing spell too and popped him inside her pocket to deal with later.

They turned around to see Kolby lying slumped on the floor. He had a small trickle of blood running down his forehead. Kaia rushed over to see if he was alright.

"I'm ok," he reassured her, "Just a little shaken. I'm sorry, he escaped."

"What happened?" Catherine asked.

"I saw him trying to make a run for the door, so I tried to fight him off with my sword. He came at me with the fireplace poker and hit me over the head. I fell down and he ran out the door. I was so dazed I didn't even see which way he went. I'm so sorry."

"Don't worry," Kaia said kindly. "We'll get him later. Let's go rescue our parents."

They ran down the corridor to the end and found the stone stairwell that led down to the dungeons. It got darker and darker as they went further down the stairs. Eventually it was so black that they had to stop. Isadora whispered "Illuminate!" As she said the word an orb of light appeared in her palm which she pushed upwards so that it hovered in the air above them lighting the way.

With the orb, they were able to move much quicker and found the dungeons quickly. They moved down the row of cells with big wooden doors chained shut trying to catch sight of King Alexander and Queen Theodora. After running up and down for what seemed like ages, Kaia's impatience got the better of her and she bellowed "MUM! DAD!"

Kolby, Catherine and Isadora froze, worried that Kaia's shouts would alert some kind of secret guard, but nobody came. Kolby, Isadora and Catherine joined in and started calling out for the King and Queen. Kaia searched frantically through the cells but could find no sign of her mum and dad. Suddenly Kolby came up to her and grabbed her by the arm. "Ssshhh!" he hissed. "I think I heard something."

They were quiet and listened hard but could only hear faint noises and they weren't sure if they were coming from a cell or from the chaos outside.

"I'll handle this," Catherine said. She raised her hand up and out the tip of her index finger came a huge cone shaped object. Catherine took it and inserted the small part into her ear and listened.

"It's an amplification device," Isadora whispered to Kaia and Kolby. It will help her to isolate the sounds and see if it is the King and Queen who are replying."

Catherine listened hard for a few minutes then clicked her fingers and the device disappeared. "They can hear us but they are two floors below us in the cells down there. Come on, let's go."

The four of them charged off down the next two flights of stairs and finally found the cell where the King and Queen were being kept. There was an invisible barrier, almost like a glass wall that all of them collided with. They picked themselves up and dusted themselves off and turned to look at Catherine.

"How are we going to get through?" Kolby asked.

"I've got this," Catherine said. "Isadora I will need your help. You need to cast a protection spell at exactly the same time as I cast the demolition spell. Our timing has to be exact or we will all be shredded by the shards of glass."

Isadora nodded grimly. She hated being under pressure. She was always so scared she would mess up. Catherine nodded to Isadora and they both took up position. "On the count of three," Catherine instructed, "One, two, three."

Both cast their spells. Kaia and Kolby looked up and saw the glass wall shatter. They heard the tinkling sounds as the glass fell all around them but they didn't feel a thing. They were protected underneath an invisible umbrella that kept them safe. They all walked forward feeling the glass shards crunch under their feet and came to stand in front of a huge wooden door. Inside the wooden door they could see a second thick steel door.

"Goodness," said Kaia. "They certainly weren't taking any chances of my parents escaping were they?"

"Well they had to be careful," said Isadora.

"Why?" Kaia asked. "Well because of your mother's magic." Catherine replied. "That's where you get your abilities from Kaia. Your mum has them too. They would have had to keep her secure and in a weakened state, much like your other family did to Isadora when they removed her amulet, otherwise she would have just blasted a hole in the wall and walked out."

"Wow!" Kaia exclaimed. "That's pretty cool."

"And as you know already Kolby," Catherine continued for Kaia's benefit. "Your dad was a fearless warrior and brave soldier. That's where you get your fighting talents from. Once we free your parents, I will cast a strengthening spell on both of them as I am not sure what kind of a state we are going to find them in. We need them strong and fit in case we have to fight our way out of here. I don't know if King Mordor made it out of the castle or if he was able to call for reinforcements. There is no way to know what will meet us when we get back up to the court yard."

Isadora stepped forward and blasted the thick heavy padlock that was on the wooden door and then they all looked at Catherine expectantly. The steel door was a solid wall of steel from the roof to the floor. It looked like it had been embedded into the stone recently as the steel was still very new.

"Maybe they tried to escape or something?" Kaia said, "So King Mordor reinforced their prison."

"Probably," Catherine agreed, "But there will be no getting through that without some very powerful magic and I think it should be you that frees them Kaia."

Kaia looked alarmed. "Me? But I don't know any powerful magic and I have never really had to use any yet – well not for something important anyway. What if I do the wrong thing or say the wrong word?" She was looking so panicked that Catherine came up to her and took her hand kindly.

"No you won't," Catherine agreed. "You won't be able to get through the steel door, but you do know enough to blast a hole through the stones. Come on, you can do this."

"Yeah," said Kolby. "Set them free Kaia."

"It should be you, Kaia dear," Isadora said coming up to stand next to her.

Kaia looked at Kolby and took all the strength she needed from her brother. She squared off her shoulders determinedly and shouted, "Mum, dad, get back and take cover! I'm going to blast a hole through the wall."

She aimed her wand and the stone and in a strong clear voice said, "*Obliterato!*"

A blue jet shot out of her wand and hit the stone. The sound of the stone wall exploding was deafening. When the dust from the spell had settled, there in front of them was a perfect hole, big enough for them to climb inside to her parents. She ran forward and clambered through the hole with Kolby and the others following close behind her. They saw the King and Queen huddled in an embrace in the corner of the cell hanging on to one another for dear life. They were filthy and thin, a mere shadow of what they used to be.

Alexander looked up at his son and daughter with so much love in his eyes that Kaia thought her heart was going to burst. He had not uttered a single word to her in all her life, yet in that look she could tell just how much she was loved. "You came," he croaked out. 'We were beginning to give up hope. It's been a year since the twins turned thirteen."
"We ran into some difficulty Your Majesty," Catherine said, "But we're here now and we are going to reclaim your kingdom. I'm going to cast a strengthening spell on you and Queen Theodora now so you will be strong enough to fight, if necessary."

"My dearest Teddy," Alexander said, looking down at the small frail body cradled limply in his arms. "She is very weak. This has all been so hard for her."

215

He looked up at Kolby and Kaia. "The worst part has been being separated from you two for so long. When she learned that Isadora and Catherine had gone through the portal with you without her, I thought the grief would kill her."

Kaia stepped forward and spoke to her father for the first time fighting hard to keep the tears from flowing. "We are here now and we will never be apart again."
"We still need to get the Kingdom back and we shouldn't waste any more time in case King Mordor has somehow been able to call for reinforcements," said Catherine in a business-like voice.

She began to wave her hands and chant and Kaia watched in disbelief as Catherine's own hands extended into a pair of golden hands. The golden hands picked up Theodora gently and held her in the air as Isadora walked forward towards her. She rummaged in her pockets and pulled out three crystals. A green one, a red one and a golden one.
She turned to Catherine and said, "which one should we use?"

"She is weaker than I thought," Catherine replied, "We had better use all of the healing crystals. I don't want any more unfortunate incidents. Let's start with the red one for mental healing."

Isadora held up the red crystal in her hand and began circling Theodora. Both she and Catherine were chanting a spell and as Kaia and Kolby watched an arc of red light began to shine out of the crystal. It enveloped Theodora and held her in a bubble. Next Isadora did the same thing with the green crystal which was for physical healing. A green bubble now surrounded the red one. Each bubble was turning around in the opposite direction and if Kaia hadn't been so scared that the spell wouldn't work she would have thought the effect was beautiful. Her mother was still limp and lifeless and Kaia was so scared that after all they had all been through she was going to be too weak to be saved. She clutched Kolby's hand for support and he looked down at her with worried eyes. His jaw was set tight and he was white as a sheet.

Next Isadora took out the golden crystal and held it up in her hands. As they said the magic words, tiny golden

217

butterflies flooded out of the crystal. They flew through the red and green bubbles and began to settle themselves all over Theodora's body until she was entirely covered. Catherine walked up to where Theodora was being held by the golden hands and said,

"Awaken O Queen. Let the butterflies breathe new life into you. Emerge from your cocoon strong, rested and healthy."

She said this over and over again, until finally Theodora's body began to move. She wriggled and writhed and arched her back as the butterflies fluttered all over her renewing her with fresh life and energizing her body, mind and spirit. Kaia stood transfixed watching the process. It was like watching someone be reborn.

Suddenly Theodora arched her back violently and Kaia jumped with shock and worry. She stretched out her arms and broke through the red and green bubbles just like a butterfly bursts out of its cocoon and Kaia looked into her mother's eyes for the very first time. She was the most beautiful woman Kaia had ever seen. Theodora walked over and gathered Kolby and Kaia in a huge hug while Catherine and Isadora cast a strengthening spell on Alexander. Since he didn't have magical abilities it was a much simpler process and just a few short minutes later Catherine came to Theodora and said, "We have to go now Your Majesty. I'm sorry."

Theodora nodded and gave her children one last hug. "Do we have any idea what we are up against when we get up there?" she asked Catherine and Isadora.

Catherine gave her a brief run-down of what had been going on when they came down to the dungeons to rescue them, but admitted that they had no idea what they would be facing once they got to the castle courtyard.

"Oh well," Theodora said. "No use dilly dallying then. Let's get up there and take a look."

"My brave and fearless Teddy," Alexander said affectionately as he hugged his children. "Still as ready as ever to dive into the action."

Theodora smiled at her husband. I'm just eager to get to know my children. I have missed out on so much."

219

Kolby handed his father his spare sword and they began their ascent to the courtyard with Catherine and Isadora leading the way, wands at the ready.

***

What a sight greeted them when they emerged into the sunshine!

The dragons had somehow rounded up all King Mordor's forces and had them imprisoned in a circle of flames. The dragons stood guard around the fire jail as an extra precaution in case someone decided to try make a run for it. The drawbridge to the castle had been lowered and there were scores of people, faeries, gnomes and rebel goblins streaming through the gates. Theodora and Alexander recognized them at once. They were their loyal supporters who had gone into hiding over the past thirteen years. A few of them were the soldiers from the war who had managed to evade capture on that fateful day all those years ago when King Mordor took over the castle. Theodora felt tears well up in her eyes as she realized that all these people had remained faithful to her husband's regime despite the personal danger to them.

The emotional moment was broken when Kaia got the giggles. She clutched her sides and laughed out loud uncontrollably. Catherine, Isadora, Kolby and her parents looked at her with shock.

"Kaia," Isadora snapped. "This is not appropriate behaviour."

"What on earth has gotten into you," Kolby said.

"The stress has finally made her crack," Catherine said.

Theodora and Alexander exchanged a worried glance. They had just gotten their daughter back and did not want to have to face the possibility that the stress of everything had caused her to go mad.

"Kaia?" her mother said quietly, "Kaia my dear child, tell me what's wrong."

But Kaia just carried on laughing. After what seemed like endless minutes Kaia managed to raise her arm and gesture towards the far corner of the courtyard. They followed her gaze and they too got the giggles, for there was Billow and dangling from his mouth by the seat of his pants was King Mordor. He was writhing and screaming and struggling to get free of Billow's grasp. Billow sat calmly while his victim wriggled around and every so often gave the Evil King a swat with his claw which caused King Mordor to erupt into a fresh round of screaming and shouting. It was such a comical sight and Kaia had not been able to control herself when she had seen it.

King Alexander was the first to compose himself, and he instructed the others to do the same.

"Dragon!" he yelled.

"His name is Billow," Kaia said with a heavy sigh.

King Alexander looked at Kaia curiously, he was not used to being interrupted and looked a little gruff, but then his wife laid a hand on his arm and he smiled at Kaia.

"Ok then, Billow," he said again. "Would you bring that vermin over here please?"

Billow ambled over and dropped Mordor at King Alexander's feet. King Alexander immediately put the tip of his sword blade over Mordor's heart. Mordor began to cry and beg and plead for his life.

"I see you are only brave when backed by an army," King Alexander said. "When you have to face me alone, you are nothing but a yellow bellied coward."

"I'm sorry sir. Your Majesty. Spare me and I will spend forever serving you." Mordor begged.

It was so quiet in the courtyard, you would have heard a pin drop. Nobody dared to move or even breathe. Everyone was certain that King Alexander would behead Mordor for all that he had done.

"Killing you would be easy," Alexander told Mordor. "No, I am not going to kill you."

"Oh thank you, thank you Your Majesty," Mordor grovelled, "I will not disappoint you. You will not be sorry."

"Killing you would simply make me as you are," King Alexander told him. "I am nothing like you, so you may live. BUT you WILL live out your days in servitude of the regime you tried to destroy."

"I'll do anything you ask," said Mordor.

"Get onto your knees," King Alexander instructed.

Mordor obeyed, he pulled himself forward and bowed his head.

"Catherine, please come here," Alexander said.

Catherine came and stood next to her King. "I am not taking any chances with this rogue in his human form. I do not trust his empty promises of servitude one bit."

"What will you have me do?" Catherine attentively asked.

Alexander leaned forward and looked down on Mordor "I want you to use the strongest magic you have to turn him into a beast of burden, so he knows what true servitude is. I wish you to transform him into a donkey."

Mordor's eyes widened in horror and he began shaking his head violently. As he tried to get to his feet, Kolby stepped forward and placed his sword to his throat.

"Just give me a reason," he said with contempt.

Alexander placed a hand on his son's sword arm. "Settle down my boy. He is not going anywhere."

Mordor whimpered and sobbed and pleaded but didn't dare to try and move again.

King Alexander then looked Mordor straight in the eyes and commanded, "I hereby sentence you to a lifetime of servitude as a donkey. You will work the royal lands and be passed down from farmer to farmer for the rest of all eternity. You will not be able to die. For all you have done, I think you have gotten off pretty lightly."

He gestured to Catherine to begin her spell and once he was transformed Mordor let out a bleat of despair. King Alexander called out to the crowds for his old farm hand to come forward and he presented him with Mordor the donkey. "Work him hard," was all he said as he handed the farmer the rope around Mordor's neck.
"Dad?" Kaia said.

King Alexander looked at her and his eyes filled with tears at the simple word that meant so much. "Yes Kaia," he finally managed. "What is it?"

She pulled the half rat half sorcerer out of her pocket and held it up by his long beard. "What are we to do with them?"

"Mmmmmm," he replied and looked at Catherine and Isadora, who had pulled her rat sorcerer out of her pocket too. "Any ideas ladies?" he asked.

"Oh I have a few ideas," Catherine said with a raised eyebrow. "But none are very nice!"

"Well I think both of them deserve a little less nice,'" he said with a wink. "Go ahead and weave your magic."

Catherine went over to Isadora and the two of them buried their heads in serious consultation. Kaia tapped her foot impatiently while she waited for them to reach their verdict. Finally Catherine stepped forward and addressed the King.

"We think that being rats suits them so much that we would like permission to complete the transformation. We will keep them locked up in a magical cage with a wheel on which they will spend their days running. The cage will be made of steel which will be far too strong for them to try chew through. However, since they are known to be very crafty characters we have decided to add an extra layer of security."

Catherine and Isadora smiled at one another as they looked at everyone's expectant faces. Kaia most especially looked as if she was going to burst from the anticipation. "If they should touch the bars of the cage or try to escape somehow, they will receive a shock so strong that they will be unconscious for a week. Each shock they receive will weaken their hearts so if they repeatedly try to escape, it will eventually kill them. If they behave they can live out their lives as rats."

King Alexander chuckled. "I love it!" he said. "I've always quite fancied the idea of a palace pet and now we have two. Make it so, dear Catherine."

As Catherine and Isadora set about their work, King Alexander called out to the crowd for any of his soldiers to come forward. A sparse crowd of men came forward.

"My loyal and brave warriors," he began. "I thank you for remaining true to me through these dark years. I trust you are all ready to resume your previous positions?"

They all nodded eagerly.

"Right," he said. "Then the first order of business is to go down into the dungeons and free your comrades who were imprisoned alongside us in the war. We need to make some space for Mordor's army to spend some time behind bars." He finished while gesturing to those being held in the fire circle.

"And now if you will all excuse us, I am going inside the castle with my beautiful family. We have a lot of catching up to do."

The crowd erupted into cheers and whoops of joy filled the air as Kaia, Kolby, Theodora and Alexander made their way inside the castle and shut the big wooden doors behind them.

Chapter 8

The next few weeks went by in a blur of activity. There was much to do in preparation for Kaia's coronation ceremony. Not to mention that the castle needed to be repaired where the dragon fire had damaged it. Queen Theodora was on a redecorating mission and was determined to erase all traces of King Mordor from the castle. She did this in close consultation with Kaia as technically it was to be her castle in a few weeks.

Kaia had enjoyed being allowed to choose her own bedroom décor and had fun experimenting with different colours and arrangements before deciding – of course it was all done with magic by Catherine and Isadora. In the end she had settled on a relatively plain bedroom. She hadn't quite processed that she was royalty and still wasn't used to the idea that she could have absolutely anything she wanted.

She and Kolby had to attend royal classes every day with the King and Queens's old royal advisors to prepare them fully for what was to come after the coronation and what would be expected of them. Kaia knew she was going to have to be extra careful to remember her manners and try her best to be ladylike. She was still getting used to walking and moving around in dresses. She had never even seen such beautiful clothes before and had never in her wildest dreams imagined having the opportunity to wear them.

Kaia was thriving being part of a 'normal' family and especially loved mealtimes where they all gathered around the table, sharing a meal and talking about their day. Kaia had never felt so loved in her whole life and spending time with her family was her absolute favourite thing to do.

She and Kolby were inseparable and they often went to visit Billow who had been welcomed into the mountain clan with open arms. Kaia had been so glad that he could go and live with Thor, because he was so big now that to have him live in the castle with her would have required some serious remodelling. King Alexander and Queen

Theodora had requested a meeting with Thor shortly after Mordor had been overthrown and they were well on their way to restoring the relationship between humans and dragons.

Kaia often thought back to her life before and it seemed like it had all happened to another person. She would never forget what Endor, Iosaf and her siblings had forced her to endure, but it no longer consumed her as much as it had before. She remembered the day Endor had locked her and Isadora up in the attic and how hopeless she had felt. She had never imagined things would work out as well as they had. She was just so completely and totally happy now and couldn't imagine anything upsetting the wonderful life she now enjoyed.

The day before the coronation ceremony her mother came to see her. "Kaia, I need to talk to you about the ceremony tomorrow. There is a part of it that nobody has told you about and I would like you to be prepared," Theodora told her.

"What is it mum?" Kaia said with a smile. She couldn't imagine what could be warranting her mother's serious expression.

"Come and sit here by me on the bed," Theodora said patting the quilt next to her. Kaia went over and joined her mother on the bed. Theodora took her hand and gave it a squeeze. She looked as though she was steeling herself to tell Kaia something awful and Kaia began to panic. She had been so happy the last few weeks and didn't want anything to upset things.

"Well, before Mordor took over the castle, there was a tradition that was upheld by all the previous generations of royalty for as far back as can be traced," Theodora began.

"Is it going to hurt?" Kaia interrupted. "Don't worry, I can handle it. I'm stronger than I look."

Theodora looked at her daughter with a mixture of fierce pride and sadness in her eyes. "It might hurt, but not in the way you are thinking," she said honestly.

At Kaia's worried expression, Theodora decided to just get on with it. "Past generations of our family felt it important to have strong leaders – Kings and Queens who were unencumbered by their past and thus could focus on the task of leading their people. They made it standard practice that before someone could ascend the throne they had to go through a cleansing ceremony of sorts."

"Cleansing ceremony?" Kaia said. "You mean I need to take a bath?"

At this Theodora giggled. Sometimes Kaia was so wise and mature that it was easy to forget she was only fourteen and despite all she had been through, she was still young at heart.

"No no," Theodora said. "Well, you will need to bath but you will also need to cleanse your soul."

"How do you do that?" Kaia asked.

"There is a ceremony that is performed by a secret keeper. A secret keeper is a very talented sorcerer and we have managed to track down the man who took our secrets from us before we were crowned. He went into hiding after the castle fell and has remained hidden for fourteen years. He contacted your father when he heard the news that you were back and has asked for his old job back.

Your father and I spoke about it and thought that it would be a good idea for you, considering all you have been through at the hands of the people you lived with."

"Ok," Kaia said warily. "What do I need to do?"

"Before the ceremony, you will visit Maximillian. He lives here in the castle again in a completely secret wing. In that wing is a room filled with all the worst secrets of our ancestors. When you enter the wing, he will cast a spell on you that will help you to release your demons. He will hand you a glass orb with an opening on the one side. Into it you will whisper all your secrets and then the orb will be sealed forever and Maximillian will keep it locked away under strong enchantments so that your demons may never affect you again. Your soul will be free of the past – although you will never forget."

Theodora's eyes filled with tears and they spilled down her cheeks. "Mum, what's wrong?" Kaia said.

"Kaia, my precious, strong amazing girl. You have no idea how guilty I feel for all you have had to endure. I wish I could have protected you from all the pain and hardships. I never wanted you to suffer like that." Theodora said wiping the tears off her cheeks.

"I know mum," Kaia said, "But everything I have been through has made me what I am today. I think I will be a better Queen because I have lived as a commoner. I know the hardships ordinary people face and I will work harder to make a better life for our people because I understand what they go through."

"You are going to make an unbelievable Queen," her mother told her sincerely. "The people are truly going to love you."

"Mum," Kaia said, "There is something else."

"What is it my darling?" her mum said.

"I need Kolby," Kaia told her. "I need him with me to help me rule. I can't do it by myself. He is such a natural because he was raised as royalty. We are a team and we need to do this together."

Theodora thought for a minute. This was most unusual. Most Kings and Queens wanted all the power for themselves. She had never met anyone who wanted to share it before and it just made her all the more proud.

"Well as you know the law dictates that only you may be crowned," her mother began.

"Yeah, yeah, I know," Kaia said rolling her eyes.

"BUT," her mother continued, "the Queen does have the discretion to choose her own advisor and there is no reason or law against giving that role to your brother. How involved you wish to make him in decisions is entirely up to you. If he agrees of course."

Kaia jumped up and gave her mother a hug. "That's great news!" she said. "I'm going to go tell him right now!"

Theodora watched her daughter skip out the room to go find her brother and thought she had never been so happy in her entire life.

***

The day of the ceremony dawned sunny and bright and Kaia woke up with mixed emotions. This was the first day of the rest of her life. She joined her family for breakfast and was quieter than usual, knowing that after breakfast she was due to visit Maximillian. She wasn't sure what to expect from the process and was feeling a little anxious. She didn't eat as much as usual and when she was finished excused herself to go off to the secret wing.

She stood outside the door and took a deep breath. As she raised her hand to knock, the door was opened and she stood facing a short man with a round face. He had grey curls peeping out of a red hat and wore purple pants and an orange tunic. She had not been expecting such a sight and the shock was clearly obvious on her face because Maximillian said, "Don't worry, everyone expects someone different for such a serious job."

That broke the ice and Kaia felt instantly at ease. She entered the room and looked around. There was a glass cabinet filled with orbs guarding the secrets of all the kings and Queens of Cypathia that had come before her. He pointed to a large purple cushion in the idle of the floor. "Let's get started."

Kaia sat down on the cushion and waited. For once she was at a loss for words. Maximillian came to her and handed her an orb, showing her the opening. "Now my dear, I am going to cast the spell on you and you are to whisper everything that weighs heavily on your heart into that orb. The spell will tell the orb when you are done and it will automatically seal, locking all your demons inside forever. I shall leave you now so you can have some privacy."

He walked around her waving his wand and she felt a squeezing around her heart, almost like the spell was trying to push the demons out of her. She heard the door click closed behind her as Maximillian left the room and she began to talk into the orb. The more she spoke the easier it became and she spilled everything into the orb. She spoke of so much hurt and pain that she felt sure the orb would shatter in her hands from being so full of all that had happened to her. But the orb stayed intact and after what felt like hours, the hole in the orb sealed over and shut.

Maximillian came back into the room and took the orb from her without saying a word. He walked over to the cabinet, waved his wand to open it and placed her orb inside alongside all the others. "You may go now Kaia," he said, "You are ready to be Queen. Good luck."

Kaia stood up and walked to the door. As she left the secret room she felt strangely empty and light. It was as if she had been wiped clean of all the bad and emptied of all the hurt so that there was space now for all the happiness that was to come. She made her way back to her room to begin getting ready for the ceremony.

***

As was tradition, the future Queen was only to enter the coronation room once everyone was assembled. Alfrida came to tell her that it was time and she was to follow her to the room where the ceremony was to take place. The main hall of the castle was packed to bursting. All of Cypathia had come to celebrate the end of Mordor's rule and to welcome the new Queen. When Kaia entered the room there was a deadly silence. It was as if everyone had stopped breathing. For a moment, she thought maybe she had done the wrong thing or come in at the wrong time, but then Theodora came up to her, gave her a kiss on the cheek and said, "Kaia, I have never seen you look so beautiful."

Gone was the dirty waif-like girl and in her place was a magnificent young woman who was strikingly beautiful. It was as if releasing all the pain of her past had allowed her inner beauty to shine though finally. She was positively glowing both inside and out. Her father came to kiss her as did Kolby and the four of them walked to the edge of the podium to present the new Queen to the people.

As Kaia reached the front, the crowd erupted into cheers and Kaia gave a small shy wave. She was taken to sit on the throne where her mother removed her own crown and placed it on her head and her father handed her the royal sceptre. Alexander turned to the crowds and announced, "I present to you, Queen Kaia of Cypathia."

The crowd went wild. Kaia sat there a little stunned by all the attention but could not stop smiling. Her father motioned to the crowds for quiet and began to speak. "I have never had a happier or prouder moment in my life than now. My daughter, I know you will rule these lands with grace and kindness."

He turned back to the people of Cypathia. "As you all know, there were portals opened that have allowed people to travel between the realms. Whilst peace has been restored, we must not get complacent in our safety and security. We have tried to destroy these portal passages, but have not been able to remove them completely. This means that anyone can travel freely through the portals to other realms and this obviously poses a security risk should there ever be a day where someone like Mordor plots to overthrow us again. Therefore with the help of my trusted magical advisor and dear friend Catherine, she has created a ring that will control access through these portal passages. Entry into Cypathia will be entirely at the discretion of the new Queen."

Kaia looked stunned. She had known nothing about this. Alexander turned to face his daughter.

"You must wear this ring always and use your wisdom when granting access to our kingdom," he said.

He walked over to her and knelt down before her. Taking her right hand in his, he slipped the ring onto her slim finger. It fit perfectly. "Catherine will show you how it works later," he whispered to her.

She smiled down at her father, but then a skirmish in the crowd caught the corner of her eye. She looked up and saw a group of people trying to push their way through the crowd. The people were not happy with late comers trying to force their way closer to the front and there were a few angry voices. Kaia looked closely and could not believe her eyes with what she saw. The audacity!

"Dad, there is something I need to take care of now. Is that ok? My first task as the new Queen?" she asked tentatively.

"Go ahead daughter. The kingdom is now yours," he replied.

Kaia stood up from the throne and walked to the edge of the podium. She addressed the crowd in a loud clear voice. "Let those people through," she demanded.

Everyone froze. The people who had been trying to push their way forward stopped at once and tried to take cover.

"I have seen you. There is no point in trying to hide. You have obviously come here for a reason so come forward and address me," Kaia demanded.

The crowd parted to make way for the people and very sheepishly Endor, Iosaf and Kaia's six siblings came forward through the throngs of people until they were directly in front of the new Queen – the child whose life they had made a misery, the child they had abused and neglected. None of them looked up but kept their heads bowed, eyes fixed firmly to the floor.

"Look at me," Kaia commanded. "And tell me what you are doing here."

It was Endor who looked up first. The look on her face was the same look of hatred that Kaia had known growing up except now there was something extra. There was jealousy, rage, and resentment. Endor just scowled at her but said nothing.

"Iosaf?" Kaia asked, looking at the man who had been her father. "Why have you come here?"

"We came to see if the rumours were true," he finally admitted. "We had heard that you were going to be crowned Queen, but none of us could believe that you were really royalty. Your sister found a witch who gave us passage through the portal to come and see for ourselves."

"I see," said Kaia. She looked Endor square in the eyes with a look of steel. "You know I could have the lot of you beheaded for treason?" she said calmly.

Her siblings looked at each other horror struck and began to squabble amongst themselves.

"You see I told you it was a mistake to come here."

"She hasn't changed."

"Still a hateful creature," Pricilla snarled through clenched teeth.

"SILENCE!" shouted Kaia.

The eight of them kept quiet but Kaia could see them shaking and quivering. Secretly she took a little delight in knowing that finally she had the upper hand over them, but since she had sealed her demons inside the orb, she no longer felt the burning desire to get revenge on them for all they had done to her. Perhaps a week ago she would have ordered their executions without blinking an eye, but Maximillian's spell had changed her inside forever. Also she knew that she had to act carefully now. This was her first act as the Queen of the Realm and would set the tone for her entire reign. Did she really want to execute them out of revenge and have her people loyal to her simply out of fear or did she rather want them loyal to her because she had earned their respect as a good leader.

Kaia took a few minutes to consider her options and while she thought her eldest sister began to cry. She was shaking uncontrollably and shuffled forward slightly. "Please Kaia," she said, "I spent much of your life out of the house. I didn't do anything to you. I have young children. Please have mercy," she begged as she fell to her knees.

"That is true," Kaia said with an exasperated sigh. "You didn't do anything to me, but did you do anything FOR me either? Did you ever try to help? Did you ever offer any kind of support? No! You too turned your back on me knowing what the rest of them were doing. In my eyes, that is no better than them. What is worse now, is that you are willing to allow the rest of your blood to endure whatever fate I order and all you are interested in is saving your own skin. That is not what family does! "

Shame-faced, her once sister skulked back to stand with the rest of her family upset that her pleas had not worked.
"I could order you executed, but luckily for all of you I am not cruel, nor will I ever stoop to your level where I torture another human being simply for my own enjoyment. And believe me, after all you have done to me, I am sure I would enjoy watching you all suffer. Since I escaped from your rotten clutches, I have learnt what love is. I have learnt what it means to have a family and I have learnt forgiveness."

At this, her old 'family' seemed to perk up and didn't look quite so stricken anymore.

Kaia noticed this and immediately got stern again. "Forgiveness DOES NOT mean I will EVER forget what you did. You will ALL be punished – just not by death. That would be too easy. Knowing what kind of people you are, I think it would torture you far more to live out your days knowing who I am and the life I now have, despite your best efforts to destroy me. I have emerged stronger than I ever thought possible and in part that is because of you. So before I hand down your punishment I would firstly I would like to thank you."

At this there was a collective murmuring through the assembled crowd. Endor looked like she was going to burst with rage. She did not ever want to be responsible for doing anything that had positively benefited Kaia.

"Yes, Endor," Kaia said, clearly relishing Endor's discomfort. "Without you, I would never have become who I am today. I stand here, fearless, because nothing could be worse than what I had to endure at your hands. I stand here strong, because if you couldn't break me, then nobody can and I stand here compassionate, because I actually feel sorry for you, for all of you. What kind of people try to break a small child just to make themselves feel better?"

Kaia paused for effect. Her old family had the grace to look thoroughly ashamed of themselves.

"So I will allow you to live but there are conditions. You shall be escorted out of Cypathia now by my brother Kolby and you must never return or try to contact me again. You will stay in Herecia and never darken my Kingdom as long as any of you shall live. Do I make myself clear?"

Seven of the eight of them nodded. Endor looked murderous, too stunned to speak. She could not believe that this had ended up being Kaia's fate. That she should end up being the Queen with the power to banish her forever.

"Endor?" Kaia questioned. "Do you agree to my terms?"
Kolby had already begun making his way down the stairs with his knights to escort them back to the portal entrance.

The last thing Endor wanted to do was to agree. She felt such a fool in front of all these people but she knew she could do nothing. If she tried to oppose Kaia now, she would likely end up with her head on a spike. She nodded with a complete lack of enthusiasm, without saying a word or looking at Kaia.

Kaia decided to allow the gesture of disrespect as she knew that Endor was not capable of having good manners. She simply cleared her throat and said, "Since we are all in agreement, be gone the lot of you. The people of Cypathia have a coronation party to enjoy."

Kolby nodded in agreement and escorted Endor, Iosaf and the rest of the family out of the hall while the crowd erupted into a chant of "Long live Queen Kaia!"

Kaia knew that there was no worse punishment than for Endor to have to hear that. She turned away from the crowd to face her mother and father and asked nervously, "how did I do?" Both Alexander and Theodora enveloped Kaia in a hug. Alexander's once strong six foot, twenty stone frame was now a slip of a man. Nonetheless, his hugs were still strong, loving and protective. Alexander whispered, "you handled that perfectly."

"I am so proud of you," Theodora said and took her daughter by the hand to lead her out of the coronation hall and to the banquet and ballroom which dazzled with bright shimmering lights where the festivities were to take place. Kaia got goose bumps when she stood in the ballroom, dressed in a beautiful cream dress with a fur lined hood. The feel of the soft fur next to her face reminded her of Billow's soft white feathers. Her goose bumps increased when she realised that this was what she had dreamed of her whole life. The family that she had dreamed of, the home she had dreamed of and especially the love she waited her whole life for.

Kaia walked hand in hand with her mother, letting out a sigh of relief, finally happy, finally feeling loved.

Cypathia. The most perfect Kingdom to ever exist.

Made in the USA
Charleston, SC
22 November 2015